UNDER THE
SMOKESTREWN SKY

AS A. DEBORAH BAKER

THE UP-AND-UNDER SERIES

Over the Woodward Wall
Along the Saltwise Sea
Into the Windwracked Wilds
Under the Smokestrewn Sky

AS SEANAN McGUIRE

Dusk or Dark or Dawn or Day
Deadlands: Boneyard
Dying With Her Cheer Pants On
Laughter at the Academy
Letters to the Pumpkin King

THE ALCHEMICAL JOURNEYS SERIES

Middlegame
Seasonal Fears

THE WAYWARD CHILDREN SERIES

Every Heart a Doorway
Down Among the Sticks and Bones
Beneath the Sugar Sky
In an Absent Dream
Come Tumbling Down
Across the Green Grass Fields
Where the Drowned Girls Go
Lost in the Moment and Found

Seanan McGuire's Wayward Children, Volumes 1–3 (boxed set)
Be Sure: Wayward Children, Books 1–3

THE OCTOBER DAYE SERIES

Rosemary and Rue
A Local Habitation
An Artificial Night
Late Eclipses
One Salt Sea
Ashes of Honor
Chimes at Midnight
The Winter Long
A Red-Rose Chain
Once Broken Faith
The Brightest Fell
Night and Silence
The Unkindest Tide
A Killing Frost
When Sorrows Come
Be the Serpent

TOR PUBLISHING GROUP

New York

UNDER THE SMOKESTREWN SKY

A. Deborah Baker

UNDER THE SMOKESTREWN SKY

Copyright © 2023 by Seanan McGuire

All rights reserved.

A Tordotcom Book
Published by Tom Doherty Associates / Tor Publishing Group
120 Broadway
New York, NY 10271

www.tor.com

Tor® is a registered trademark of Macmillan
Publishing Group, LLC.

The Library of Congress Cataloging-in-Publication Data
is available upon request.

ISBN 978-1-250-84847-5 (hardback)
ISBN 978-1-250-84848-2 (ebook)

Our books may be purchased in bulk for promotional, educational, or business use. Please contact your local bookseller or the Macmillan Corporate and Premium Sales Department at 1-800-221-7945, extension 5442, or by email at MacmillanSpecialMarkets@macmillan.com.

First Edition: 2023

Printed in the United States of America

0 9 8 7 6 5 4 3 2 1

FOR JOSHUA, AND FOR CASEY.
ALL THE ALCHEMY YOU EVER NEEDED
WAS IN YOU FROM THE START.

UNDER THE
SMOKESTREWN SKY

ONE

REMINDERS AND DEFINITIONS

When last we came together, you and I, we spoke to each other of middles, which are vast and tangled and sticky. They can cling to your feet and drag you down, such that you find yourself eternally wandering in the center of a story, trapped with no way back to where you began, and even less hope of a way forward to the finish. We spoke of beginnings and their commonalities, and indeed, we had a beginning together, side by side as we set off into story, following a path that exists only for the reader, and not for those already standing inside. This is only fair. They have access to roads that we do not; the world would be out of balance if they could reach for all of ours.

But that was then, in the dark and distant country of the past, where you and I can never go again, no matter how much we might desire it. Time is a road that only runs in one direction for all save a very fortunate few, and none of us is counted in their number. We must go onward. We must leave the middle behind, as once we left the beginning, and continue toward the high, looming cliff of the conclusion. We are almost to the end, my dears, and once we reach it, there will be no further road to follow. This story will be finished. You can go back to the beginning, should you desire, and begin anew, but as time will not start over with you, you will not see the journey the same way. You will know things. You will understand things. Only be aware that knowing and understanding may change the way you feel about the beginning, the middle, and the end. Traveling through the same story a second time is a form of alchemy. The story you have already experienced will never be available to you again. That tale is ending.

As we are approaching the last time we will be able to speak together for the first time, it seems like a kindness to remind you of what has come before, what obstacles we have overcome and what wonders we have seen, all in the reaching of this place. We are still in the country of once upon a time, after all, and it would be best to remember that as clearly as we can.

So: once, on the other side of many days and many adventures, two children lived on the same street, although they did not know it, and lived plain, pleasant, parallel lives, all unaware of the companion they had yet to meet. Their names were Avery Alexander Grey and Hepzibah Laurel Jones. Avery had no nicknames, no sweet diminutives, but called himself ever and entirely "Avery," complete in his own circle of one. Hepzibah went only and always by "Zib," and left her given name behind her, as if it were a burden too heavy to be carried on her narrow shoulders. They were both content with the worlds that they inhabited, and unaware of the other worlds existing so close outside their own.

But those worlds *did* exist, as other worlds have always existed and always will, and on a day that had seemed the same as any other, the children found themselves confronted with a series of surprises. First, a broken water main, which forced them both to walk a new route to get to school. Second, each other, two strangers staring wide-eyed and bewildered at the intruder in a territory they had always viewed as theirs alone. Surely, thought Avery, I would have noticed someone so wild and unkempt where she didn't belong! And surely, thought Zib, I would have noticed someone so pressed and polished where *he* didn't belong! In this, they still paralleled each other, as they had always unknowingly done from the beginning, even as they walked toward a wall that shouldn't have been there, blocking their passage into a forest that both of them knew, quite completely, did not and could not possibly exist.

Over the wall they went, the boy and the girl, the pressed and the rumpled, the A and the Z of our story. They did not know it, but they were already standing firmly on the improbable road, which is not always visible. This is the danger of walking a road that has opinions about where it belongs: it can move, at times, between worlds, transferring properties from one into the next, transmuting the familiar into the unforeseen. The improbable road had come to collect them, knowing them for its own, because the improbable road is one of the few things that can actually travel backward along the twisting weave of time, collecting what it needs from past and from future.

If Avery and Zib seem strange to you, only remember that they may well be children of a different time, brought backward or forward to suit the needs of a piece of opinionated pavement. If *this* is the thing which seems strange to you, perhaps you are not yet ready for the ending, and should go back to the beginning and make your way here to us again, paragraph by paragraph, page by page. Don't worry. I'll wait for you here as long as you need me to, as I always have, as I always will.

Over the wall, into the wood, and out the other side! Through the Kingdom belonging to the King of Coins, from whose hands pour wealth of every kind, gemstones without price, minerals without measure, who can woo even the stones themselves to speak! Across the frozen river that marks the border between his domain and the Kingdom of the King of Cups, who trades in cold and consequences, all the way to the borders of the Saltwise Sea!

All along the way they traveled the improbable road, which led them true if not direct, and would have taken them to the Impossible City, where stories begin and end and go on forever, had they not taken up company with Niamh, a drowned girl, who was very possible in ways that they were not, and was thus barred from the city streets.

Ah, but what *is* the Impossible City? Its shadow has stretched across everything we've shared together, all the way back to the very first word I spoke to you. It is device and destination, something to be sought and something to be denied, the storied principality of the Queen of Wands, who has yet to make an appearance in her own skin, looking through her own eyes. It must be something very grand, this city, to be Impossible and real at the same time, and more, to be something so dearly sought after and desired! It must be something grand indeed.

But we are getting there, one step at a time, and

there are still steps to be taken, still paths unfollowed yet ahead of us.

From the edges of the Saltwise Sea to the very center, from solid land to the deck of a sailing ship! Children to travelers to passengers to pirates, and finally, to the aid of the Lady of Salt and Sorrow, who had been sundered into two people for so very long that she had almost forgotten how to be herself, intact and entire. The Lady forgave them and freed them to continue onward, and so they went beneath the sea, crossing to the Kingdom of the Queen of Swords in the belly of a mosasaur, which would have seemed impossible on the other side of the woodward wall which began their entire adventure.

From there, a beach to a mountain to a mesa, winds to wishes to exchanges, and the palace of the Queen of Swords, creator of crows and thief of hearts. They learned many things while in her company, but chief among them was the name of the Crow Girl who had traveled with them almost from the beginning, who had traded her heart and her name for the freedom to fly, and had never thought to see either one of those things again. A name is a terrible, glorious thing. Once spoken, it changes everything.

Soleil, she had been called, before she gave up her heart and received a black-winged bird in exchange. Soleil, she was to be called again, as she fled the palace with Avery and Zib, with Niamh and with Jack, the son of the Queen of Swords, who wished to escape with more than just his life. So she was Soleil once more and for the first time; she was someone new, in her way, and this new person remained a mystery to all except Soleil herself, who had remembered her own identity and would now be able to chart her story by her own map once again.

From the palace to the improbable road, which now stretched like a rainbow film of oil atop the water across the heavens, bending high and carrying the fleeing children quite away. Of all their allies, the road had been the most consistent, and would remain so, at least until one of them left it for the final time.

Because that is the thing about endings, my dears, the thing you must all remember, and keep close and secret next to your own hearts, which have not been replaced with black-winged birds, but still beat strong and true: that is the thing you must hold to as the improbable road bends toward the burning Kingdom of the Queen of Wands, which has smoldered endlessly in the absence of its Queen, and would burn eternally waiting for her. Endings are where we suffer the deepest losses, where we look with critical eyes upon the toys with which we play and cast some of them aside forevermore, no longer to be pieces in our games.

Endings are where we can afford to let them go.

Keep this close and foremost in your mind, and when the moment arrives, remember that I warned you: remember that I told you from the very start that this would be so.

We have walked with Avery and Zib since the beginning. We have seen them tested and tried, seen them succeed and seen them fail, and soon, we may see one of them fall. There are many ways into the Up-and-Under. There are almost as many ways out again, and not all of them run in both directions. I will tell you this much now, to set your jangled nerves at ease: they came via the same path, and they traveled the divided, elemental lands via the same road. When they leave, however, they will each of them go alone.

Will knowing this now change how you see the story? Will it shift a part of you into the future, into the time when you have been here before and cannot see this all with fresh and open eyes? I do not know. That, my dears, is up to you.

But here and now, we have traveled past the borderless beginning and through the murky middle. We must now approach the inescapable ending, which has always been coming for us, which has always been here. We will go as Avery and Zib did, side by side and hand in hand, and I will not let you go. Unlike the children we accompany, we will return by the same road, you and I, and I will bid you a fond farewell before you turn toward other stories, other storytellers, and leave me consigned to the kingdom of the past, where I may rest a little while.

Only know that I will always have been here, and you will always have been here, and although time divides us in all other ways, we will have been here together. Hold that knowledge fast, and trust in me now, and let me lead you onward toward the final counting of our quarters. Now is where we join them, five children walking on a soap-bubble passage stretched across the sky, moving closer and closer to the burning land below.

And the children walked on.

TWO

A LAND OF ASH
AND EMBERS

As had happened at least twice before—which, in the strange and often contradictory language of childhood, had become the same as "many times before," and was on the cusp of being transmuted into "always"—Zib led the way down the arching rainbow shimmer of the road, descending toward the burning ground with each step she took. She was still wearing the too-flimsy shoes the Crow Girl had found for her at the bottom of a wardrobe in the castle of the Queen of Swords, and their soles were too slick to properly grasp the almost-untextured surface beneath them. It was thus not much of a surprise

when, between one step and the next, she began to slide, skidding downward with startling speed.

Zib cried out, a sound caught somewhere between a wail and a shout, and windmilled her arms wildly, trying to catch hold of her balance. Balance is a slippery thing, slipperier even than shoes with smooth soles: once it has skidded out of hand, it can be all but impossible to recapture.

Behind her, her companions reacted with varying degrees of distress. Avery took a step forward, reaching for her. His own shoes, which had once been new and crisp and polished to an almost-mirrored glossiness, were worn almost as smooth as her own; he felt them starting to lose traction, and stopped, stepping back again, to keep himself from tumbling after her. One of them falling was bad. Both of them falling had never once led them to anything good.

Behind him stood Niamh, the drowned girl, who was slippery and damp by nature, and had been struggling to keep her balance ever since the road began dipping down, and Soleil, who had been the Crow Girl, who might still be the Crow Girl on some level, deep below the surface of her skin, but who was currently heartsick and stuck from the revelation of her name and her heart and the woman she had been before the Queen of Swords. Neither of them moved.

Behind *them* stood the newest member of their

company, a lanky teenage boy a few years older than his companions—old enough, by the shape of him, that some people would have said he had outgrown adventures, that he was ready to settle down and devote himself to the business of becoming an adult. Those people would have been wrong in all the ways it's possible for a person to be wrong, because age alone is never what determines whether or not one has outgrown adventures. Some people are too old for adventures when they are still settled snugly in their nurseries, and others remain ready for the world to change long after they have children and grandchildren of their own, all of them seeking their way to the improbable road. Appearances alone can never tell the entire story.

Some boys his age might have been too old for adventures, but not *this* boy, with his long fingers and clever hands. He wore a suit of black feathers, similar in material, cut, and style to Soleil's dress, and his hair was a steely gray a few shades darker than his eyes. He was too sharp to be handsome, seeming almost avian in the way he moved and cocked his head to watch Zib sliding downward. He tensed, and then "almost" became actuality as he burst into a flock of gray-and-black birds.

They took to the air immediately, flying down to the road a few feet ahead of Zib, where they coalesced back into a boy, who caught her easily, only staggering a little under her weight. Zib caught her breath, heart pounding from the thrill and terror of her descent, and clung to his arm like a lifeline.

"Are you all right?" he asked.

"Yes—no—help me sit down."

Zib was already folded halfway over after his catch, and it was a simple thing for him to ease her into a sitting position on the iridescent ribbon of the road. Behind them, the other three stopped walking, Avery, Niamh, and Soleil, all in a line.

Moving fast and almost angry, Zib unstrapped the shoes and peeled the socks from her feet and moved as if to throw them over the side of the road. The boy caught her wrist before she could finish the motion. She turned to look at him, with none of the gratitude she'd carried only a moment before.

"What are you doing?"

"You're going to want something for your feet when we get to the ground, since you can't fly," he said. "More than any other Kingdom, the Kingdom of the Queen of Wands will remind you when you're not in your own element."

Zib paused. She was not particularly fond of burning. She spent her summers barefoot—her autumns, springs, and winters, too, as much as the weather allowed—and had scorched the soles of her feet often enough to know very well that she didn't like it in the least. So she relaxed her arm, and when the boy let her go, it dropped back to her side, shoes and socks still in hand.

"I'm not wearing them on the road, if it's going to let me fall like that," she said, a challenge in her voice.

"Don't tempt the road," said Niamh, her own voice urgent and her own feet bare, as they always were. Drowned girls are their own kind of person, neither fully living nor entirely dead, and they follow their own rules. Because of the way she had left the world of the fully living, she was always damp, leaving puddles behind her when she walked. Because of *that* undeniable reality, she most often refused to wear shoes. They would only fill with water, and not even a drowned girl likes to walk in soaking shoes.

But the road had left them before, when they seemed too critical of the way that it was going, or acted as if they were too good to be going where it led them. A road which has opinions about where it begins and ends can have feelings, too, and those feelings can be hurt. Upsetting the improbable road was never a good idea, especially not when it had a tendency to arrange passage through the air or along the surface of the sea. Having the road suddenly vanish under those circumstances was not only distressing but potentially dangerous! The last time one of them had upset the improbable road, they had all been dumped into the depths of the Saltwise Sea, and only the fact that the Lady of Salt and Sorrow had been willing to intervene on their behalf and send a mosa-saur to swallow them whole had kept Avery, Zib, and the Crow Girl from drowning.

Niamh would have survived. It takes more than a little dip in the ocean to kill a drowned girl. But she would have survived knowing that her friends had died while she was powerless to save them, and she would have carried that terrible weight for all the days of her everlasting life, weighing her down like rocks strapped to her ankles.

"Sorry, road," said Zib, and actually patted the transparent pavement, like she was trying to soothe an anxious horse.

Thankfully for the nerves of everyone presently on the improbable road, the ribbon of iridescence didn't whinny or rear up into her hand. Neither did it dissolve and leave them to plummet. Gingerly, Zib stood, the teen standing ready to catch her if she fell again, and resumed her trek downward, the others following close behind.

THREE

THE STORY OF JACK DAW

Let us take a moment—as this is our last outing together, it will be full of digressions, pauses to say all that need be said, times where we step away from the action to discuss some point of necessity. I hope you will not mind, my future dear one, who sits and reads or is read to but cannot be here with me now, in this hour, where I am writing the words now set before you. I hope you will forgive me for being eager, as our time together draws to a close, to be sure you understand all that I have tried to offer to you.

So let us take a moment to consider the story of Jack Daw, only son and never heir to the Queen of Swords, who knew more of making monsters than

of raising children. The Queen had the heart out of the boy before he was old enough to recognize the sound of his own name, which was for the best, as she had never granted him a name to call his own. Instead, she hung a birdcage inside his chest, and placed a jackdaw inside the birdcage, so that his body would have the knowing of how to break itself into birds and take to the skies.

She called him "Jack," after the birds he could become, and made him a Page in her Court, neither man nor monster, neither child nor corvid, but something caught forever in the middle. Unlike the Crow Girl, who had been her own person before she found herself transformed, he had never known himself to be anything other than he was. There is a power in that sort of thing not to be discounted. He had no questions about his own nature or who he was, no uncertainty as to who he would become: all those things had been answered for him, and if he didn't always like the answers, he would still live with them.

He had no choice.

Had the Queen of Swords been a better mother, had she treated Jack as anything other than a useful toy to dangle at the end of a string, he might have been less inclined to betray her. But his whole life had been a long game played by rules he could never fully understand, rules written by the woman who had first grown and then stolen his heart, as if his humanity were an apple to be plucked from a tree. Someone who has never been allowed to choose anything for themselves may make the first choice open to them, and it will not always be the choice we want them to make. So when Avery, Zib, and their companions tumbled into his mother's keeping, he began planning to betray her, if not straightaway, then as soon as he had properly made their acquaintance.

He had been a prisoner looking for an escape route for a very long time, and when he found it in a company of children who were quite clearly on a quest of some sort, who contained all the elements within their number—or seemed to, anyway; at the time, the Crow Girl was still a nameless creation of the Queen of Swords, and still seemed tied to the air. It was only when her heart was returned to her that she was revealed as a creature of fire, making Jack more important to the completion of their quarters than he could possibly have known.

Jack was not a cruel boy, nor a wicked boy, nor a mean boy, but he was still a monster. He walked through the world without a heart, and the decisions he made were based on his needs and his needs alone. You will need to remember that, as we travel onward, through the country of fire, where all is ash and ember, and never the cold can come.

Remember who our monsters are, however attractive they may seem.

But as to who his father was, he had never asked nor attempted to uncover. The man was inconsequential in the story of Jack Daw, as his mother was the Queen of the Kingdom of the Air, and her gift was in the making of monsters. Jack knew himself to be a monster, if a toothless one, and at times he thought he had never had a father at all but was entirely his mother's creation. At this point in his story, he may as well have been.

Still, he felt a strange pull toward Avery and Zib, so that when he had the opportunity to help them, he took it, seeing no other clear way through the story they were all tangled up inside. Now, as he descended toward the Kingdom of Wands, he was as tangled in their story as they were, for he could never go back to his mother's castle, and as he was known to be her creature, there was no other place in all the Up-and-Under that would have him.

Downward Jack descended, keeping pace with his companions, and the only difference between them was that he did not fear falling. The air was not quite closed to him; the wind would lift his wings, if he had need of such support.

And onward they continued.

You may be wondering why, if we could take such digressions at any time, this is the first time we have stopped the progress of the adventure to tell you someone's story. Wouldn't it have helped, after all, to know that Niamh would find the lost princess of her sunken city in the Saltwise Sea, or that the Crow Girl could recover her heart in the Kingdom of the Queen of Swords? But if that's the journey you desire, one where everything is known from the beginning, where there are no surprises, you have a way to take it. As we have already discussed, you can go back to the start at any time. Open a different book, and travel through this tale as a seasoned wanderer, not a novice stumbling along on their first adventure.

You will see, if you do this thing, how silly some characters may seem, not to know things which are, in hindsight, perfectly and absolutely clear. All the doors will have been unlocked for you, all the mysteries delivered pre-solved and ready for dissection. This is the easy way to travel through a story, and it will teach you something new, for no story is the same twice, but the largest and most foundational of its lessons will already have been imparted. They cannot be given a second time.

We take this stop for Jack when we took it for none of the others for one simple reason: he has no secrets to unravel. There is nothing about him yet unknown. He is a monster, crafted by the Queen of Swords from the boy who was her son and a flock of birds who had the misfortune to be hatched in her lands, and the only deceit he carried in the birdcage that should have held his heart was the willingness to betray his mother. To have introduced him so at the beginning of the story would have untangled little, might at most have stolen a moment of surprise. To do the same with the others, who have led more complicated lives, would have changed our understanding of them entirely.

So you see, this was not *always* a choice open to us, and we pause to do it now solely because we will not have the time to do it later.

But come, come. Back to the bending rainbow ribbon of the road, back to the five children who descend toward the burning ground with careful, mincing steps, uncertain of their welcome in this strange new land, knowing only that they can never, in this world, go back to where they were.

Onward they travel, and what happens next is a mystery to us all.

FOUR
TO THE GROUND

Reaching the place where the road bent to smooth itself over the ground, Zib hesitated. She was well known to be a reasonably fearless girl—or perhaps unreasonably, as she had a tendency to throw herself bodily into situations she would have been better off avoiding, as if she thought the world itself would catch her any time she fell—but even reasonably fearless girls can be cautious about leaping onto a bed of burning coals. The ground around the rainbow film of the road resembled nothing so much as the embers at the bottom of a campfire after a long night's burning, when most of the fuel has been consumed but the heat still lingers.

The crust atop the embers was burn-black, dark as coal, lifeless and charred. Seams ran through it like cracks in a broken mirror, and through them gleamed sparks of red and gold and even startling sapphire blue. Over it all, a thin gray film of ash clung and danced, only scarcely heavy enough to drop out of the air. More ash rained down on them from above, a constant, drifting mist that neither burnt nor choked but left Avery feeling grimy, and Zib with the distinct need to sneeze.

Jack caught her hesitation and stepped past her, down onto the flat stretch of road ahead of them. He was careful to keep his feet planted firmly on the dancing rainbows, not touching their blackened surroundings in the slightest. "The elemental lands don't normally wear their colors this close to the surface, but it's no more dangerous than the other Kingdoms," he said.

"We almost drowned in a river of mud in the Kingdom of Cups," said Zib warily. "And we *really* almost drowned in the Saltwise Sea."

"And after that, we were harried and harassed by all manner of winds and zephyrs," said Avery, not to be left out of what felt like a terribly important conversation.

"Jack's right," said Soleil. She moved up behind Avery, forcing him to step aside and let her pass or risk being knocked entirely off the road. "Every elemental land shows its nature somewhere, but the Kingdom of Wands should be . . . I don't know, a lake of lava, or a field of tiny cultivated volcanos waiting until they're big enough to transplant someplace where they can grow big and strong. It shouldn't be the whole *country*."

Like Jack, she moved past Zib, staying carefully within the bounds of the improbable road as she stepped down onto the ground.

Zib frowned. She was normally the first one to charge into any danger. It felt almost like a failing that she was one of only three left standing on the "bridge" the road had formed for them as it arced across the sky. "But it can still burn us, right?"

"All fire can burn," said Soleil, tone implying that this was something that should never have needed to be said: it was self-evident and clear. "These fires are always here. They just normally mask themselves better than this."

Zib swallowed hard and stepped down, at last, onto the road. "The ground looks just like your hair," she said. "Did you notice that?"

Soleil turned to look over the edge of the road at the smoldering ground surrounding them. "So it does," she said, almost wonderingly. "I wonder . . . is this where I came from?"

"How much do you remember?" asked Niamh, following Zib down from the bridge.

As soon as she stepped onto the ground, the road behind them shivered and disappeared, leaving them at the very beginning of what they assumed would be a safe passage through the burning plains. There was no way back for them now, if ever there had been to begin with. There was only onward, into the flames.

Soleil considered her question for almost a full minute, chewing her bottom lip between her teeth. "Something in the middle of everything and nothing," she said finally. "I remember meeting you all. I remember my name. I remember being very sad and very scared and very sure that I had no other way out of some trouble I was in, even if I can't remember what the trouble was. And I remember the Queen of Swords told me she could make it all go away, and all I had to give her was my heart." A line formed between her eyebrows as she scowled. "She made it sound like she could take my heart and still leave me with everything else. She never said she'd steal my name and my self and everything else away at the same time."

"Was the Crow Girl ever real?" asked Zib, a sudden horror sparking in her own heart, which had been risked and bruised but never stolen. The Crow Girl had been her friend—possibly her first friend in the Up-and-Under, less complicated than Avery, whose rough edges so often caught and clashed against Zib's own—and the thought that she might never have been real was a variety of pain that Zib had never dreamt of before.

The world is very skilled at the production of new ways to be hurt. The only blessing this truth carries is that whenever the world provides a new way of hurting, it provides a new way of healing as well.

"She was," said Soleil. "*I* was. I remember being her, and even if she wasn't real, the things we did together were. You were real, and you were there, and that means they really happened."

"So does that mean *we're* friends now?" asked Zib. They were standing on a thin line of rainbow road in the middle of a burning waste, and this conversation suddenly felt like the most important thing in all the world. There hadn't been much time for talking as they fled across the sky, all of them sure that the forces of the Queen of Swords would descend upon them at any moment.

But the Queen of Swords was a maker of monsters, which makes her a sort of monster in her own right, the sort who would rather hide behind someone else's teeth and claws than risk endangering herself. She was a cautious monster, and they had already defeated her in her den. When pressed, she would rather retreat than pursue.

Not every monster, when so thwarted, will pull their talons back and let their victims go. This is a truth. At the same time, many monsters became monsters out of a kind of cowardice, and cannot stand to be reminded of their own fallibility. So it was that they had been able to reach the Kingdom of Wands unchallenged, which was good, considering the challenges that still lay ahead. Monsters in the past have either been evaded or defeated, and are not necessarily a problem any longer. Monsters in the future, on the other hand . . .

With the Queen of Swords behind them and not yet in the past, there had been no time to speak of things as simple and essential as identity. What did it matter who was friends with whom when you were all about to die? Zib looked anxiously at Soleil, waiting for her answer, and no one said a word, not even Jack. The only sound was the faint susurration of the ashen flakes drifting from the sky and settling, soft as snow, on the ground around them.

Soleil screwed up her face, plainly thinking hard about Zib's question. Zib found that encouraging, in a sideways sort of way. The Crow Girl hadn't known precisely how old she was—time ran differently for birds than it did for children—and so even though she'd looked a fair few years older than Avery and Zib, it had always seemed like they were just about the same age. Older children didn't play with younger ones when they had a choice. This was a plain and simple reality of life as Avery and Zib knew it.

Adults seemed to forget this fact, maybe because

they were so very ancient and wise that a gap of a few years no longer seemed to matter to them, but when someone was eight years old, the idea of spending their time with a six-year-old would have been as unthinkable as a ten-year-old deigning to come down from the lofty heights of almost-adulthood to spend time with an eight-year-old. It had been easy, since the Crow Girl wasn't human, to pretend that the rules didn't apply to her, that she was allowed to violate them without noticing because she didn't know they were even there. Soleil, though . . .

Soleil looked like she was even older than Jack, and Jack was obviously a teenager, older even than the Crow Girl, if just as unbound by ordinary rules as she had been. Soleil was almost tall enough to be a grownup already, and she had a finished look to her features, like they had been drawn and redrawn by some unseen artist until they were almost complete. She wasn't an adult, not yet. She could see the borders of that country from where she stood. As to whether she was human or still halfway the monster the Queen of Swords had made of her, that was less than clear.

"I don't know," said Soleil, feeling her way through even that short sentence with exquisite care. "I remember that we were friends. I remember that we had so many adventures together, and I remember that the person I was liked the person you are.

But whether the person I am now is friends with the person you are now, I think we'll have to wait and see."

Somehow, that was more reassuring to Zib than a simple "yes" would have been. Adults who said "yes" to complicated questions without stopping to think about it first were all too frequently lying, because it was easier than wrestling with the complicated beast that was the truth. Zib did not particularly care for being lied to.

Niamh stepped closer, drops of water falling from her hair to the road. A few missed the road entirely and struck the ground, and the question of whether it was as hot as it looked was answered when they sizzled like they'd been flicked onto a frying pan.

"My dad says the hood of the car is hot enough to fry an egg sometimes in the summer," said Avery. "I think he's exaggerating, but I also think this ground is hot enough to fry an egg."

"So everyone will have to walk very carefully, but we can't stand here forever," said Niamh. "Even if we wanted to, the road would get tired of waiting for us, and might decide to continue on to wherever it's going."

The thought of having the road slide out from underneath their feet and leave them standing in the burning plain with nothing to protect them was bracing enough to startle the others into motion. They began to walk again, this time following the improbable road as it stretched into the distance, heading for the jagged, looming shape of the mountains that stood like black glass walls against the smoky sky.

Avery was the last to move, lingering toward the rear of the group. He turned to look back in the direction of the Kingdom of Swords, already missing the clean air and plentiful food of that open, arid place, and blanched as he saw the improbable road moving toward him as quickly as the others were moving away. It was as if it were rolling itself up, unwilling to be left behind. All too soon, Niamh's threat of the road moving on without them could become true.

Pivoting back to face the others, Avery hurried after them, the improbable road following close behind.

FIVE

THE FIREFLOWER FIELDS

They walked for what felt like miles through the blackened waste, the air growing slowly hotter and hotter around them, until Avery and Zib were sweltering in their clothes, and the moisture that always dripped from Niamh was pouring off her in buckets, leaving actual puddles on the road where she walked. Those puddles didn't last for long before they evaporated into the air, and the one time Zib had tried to double back and wet her hands, she had recoiled with a shout. The water, which had dripped from Niamh only a few seconds before, was already boiling hot, and scalded Zib's fingers.

Niamh herself was starting to look pale and

waxen, like she was running a very high fever. Jack didn't look much better. People who don't spend a lot of time around birds may not realize, but birds are delicate creatures. So many of them migrate not because they crave the pleasures of novelty or the excitement of moving house, but to escape extremes of heat and cold. For every bird that's built to survive freezing winters or searing summers, there are ten more that aren't. Ten more whose feathers will freeze or whose blood will boil in their veins. Farmers lose chickens when the summers sour. Crows drop out of the sky.

Jackdaws are hardy birds, built to scavenge and soar, but they don't do well with extreme temperatures.

Only Soleil looked entirely unbothered by the heat. She walked on, as calm in the middle of the journey as she'd been in the beginning, and it wasn't until she heard Zib's gasp from behind her that she slowed, stopped, and looked back at the younger girl.

"Yes?" she asked. "What is it?"

"You left the road," said Zib, her eyes so wide they seemed at risk of popping out of her head. She pointed at Soleil's feet with one quivering hand, apparently unable to say any more than that.

Soleil looked down, following the angle of Zib's finger. Her own eyes widened as she saw that she was standing about a foot to the left of the road, her bare feet firmly planted on the smoldering ground. With a squeak of alarm—but not of pain—she jumped back onto the road.

"I didn't mean to!" she said, voice almost frantic. She looked from Zib to Avery, wrapping her arms around herself. "I wasn't trying to— I just didn't notice when— What's happening?"

Her final question was a plaintive wail as much as anything. Jack, looking paler and more ill than ever, stepped forward and tried to take her hand, coaxing it out of the feathers of her dress.

"It's all right," he said soothingly. "My mother makes her monsters out of citizens of all the Kingdoms in the world. Perhaps you were originally born of fire, and so it doesn't seek to scorch you when you tread on it lightly."

"Perhaps," said Soleil, still looking uncomfortable. The group started moving forward again, and her feet left little black smudges on the pavement, which lasted only long enough for Niamh's dripping to wash them quite away.

"The Crow Girl always said she was a creature of the air," said Avery. "The way you divide people into elements here is quite queer to me. We don't do things like that where I come from."

"I'm sure you have some way of dividing people," said Jack. "Every place I've ever heard about has had some form of interior division. It might be the color of your skin, or your hair, or what size shoes you wear, or what languages you speak, but there's *something*. Maybe you're just too young to have seen it for what it is."

That was the first time Jack had referred to either of them as too young for something. Avery and Zib both bristled, for different reasons. Zib because she didn't like to feel as if she was being dismissed for any reason; Avery because he didn't care for Jack's breezy assumption that they were too young to have seen the way that people split themselves on lines that didn't actually exist.

"I don't think I was ever once too young for that," said Avery stiffly. "My father says that we have to be twice as good as anybody else if we want to get even half as much respect from the world, and since you're not respecting me so much right now, I guess he's right."

Jack blinked. He could tell he'd said something wrong, although he couldn't see quite what it was. "Well, here, we don't care so much about what a person looks like, or how they speak, or what species they are, or even if they're alive the same way everyone around them is. What we care about is the element you spring from."

"There are four," said Niamh, her voice only slightly stronger than Jack's. "They correspond to the four Kingdoms and monarchs, and they shape everything we are. No single person is purely one or the other. Our Kings and Queens come closest, which is why they always seem to be a bit off to the rest of us. A person isn't meant to be born entirely of one element, although it's perfectly fine for someone to be missing all or most of one. The easiest people are a blend of all four. They walk easy, breathe easy, and when they try to shape the world to suit their own ends, the world answers easy. The rest of us have to make up for our failings in other ways."

"I'm almost entirely Air," said Jack. "It comes of having a bird instead of a heart. My bones are hollow in the middle, and my flesh yearns to be cloaked in feathers. There's a spark of Fire in me, to keep my body moving and my thoughts burning, and a surprising amount of Earth, or I'd never be able to come back together after I became birds. But there's almost nothing of Water. I don't handle cold well, and if my feathers get wet, I get pulled down much too easily. I could drown before I knew I was in danger."

Avery, who remembered the drowned crows scattered around the inside of the mosasaur after their plunge into the Saltwise Sea, shivered and said nothing. Jack wasn't finished, and continued without seeming to take note of Avery's discomfort.

"I would probably have been Air no matter what, because of who my mother was, but I might have been more called to Water, or to Earth, or to any

other element. When I came of age, I could have im-
migrated to one of the other Kingdoms, or I could
have stayed where I was born and served to help us
stay unified."

"I was born of Air," said Niamh. "When I
drowned, the Water rushed in and washed everything else away. Now I'm all Water and Earth, and
very little Air, and nothing at all of Fire."

"How do people just *know* these things?" asked
Zib. "I don't have any elements in me at all, that I
know of. I'm a girl. A perfectly normal human girl."

"Ah, but human girls are made of elements," said
Jack. "Things like carbon and iron and calcium—all
manner of things. There are so many more elements
than just the four we count by."

"We would have so many Kingdoms if we counted
all the elements," said Niamh. "Some of them would
be almost too small for anyone to see, and have room
in them for maybe one or two people. There would
be so many Kings and Queens and Pages that we'd
never be able to get anything done, and the Impossible City would be bursting at the seams with trying
to hold all the embassies they'd need!"

The image had Zib giggling, until the other half of
it caught up with her and struck her giggles dead. All
the Kings and Queens they'd known so far had been
so powerful as to be barely human anymore, and their
Pages, even the gentle ones, had been creatures out of

nightmare, too made of magic and mischief to have any room left inside them for kindness or care. Filling the world with elemental countries might be fun for a moment, but when their rulers appeared, jockeying for power and position, the fun would quickly come to an end.

"So science says we're made of elements, no matter what we are," said Avery.

"Science?" asked Niamh blankly.

"Science is taking things you know are true and using tests and information to prove how true they are," said Avery. "Sometimes scientists prove that the things they know are true aren't true at all, and those are very confusing days for them."

"Are you saying that your 'science' can make people disappear?" asked Soleil, sounding horrified.

"What?" asked Avery.

"I'm Fire and Air," said Soleil. "I'm not carbon or calcium or any of those other things. I'm not Water, either, and I'm barely Earth at all. Your science would say I can't exist. If your scientists ran their tests and proved that I wasn't real, would I just pop like a soap bubble?"

"I don't think so," said Avery, and now it was his turn to sound horrified, and quite confused.

The land had begun to change around them as they walked, still blackened and seamed with red, but now dotted with large boulders and what looked like patches of little white flowers with white centers. Some of them were almost close enough to the road to touch. Zib looked at them longingly as the group walked on, wishing she could walk over to the flowerbeds in the blistered ground—flowerbeds that couldn't possibly have existed.

Behind her, the conversation about science continued, Avery trying to explain it to the others in a way that wouldn't alarm or confuse, Jack and Soleil asking the occasional question, and Niamh following pale and wilting at the rear. They were so thoroughly distracted that when Zib suddenly pointed to the horizon and shouted, "Look!" none of them had noticed whatever it was she was pointing at.

One by one, they followed the angle of her finger, squinting at the sky, and for a moment, they saw nothing out of place. It was just an ordinary sky, streaked with smoke and grayish clouds. Then Avery blinked, and saw that one of those clouds had somehow managed to escape the smoke that stained the others, remaining as white and pristine as fresh-fallen snow. Another blink, and the cloud wasn't a cloud at all but an owl soaring toward them with steady beats of its massive white wings.

Avery took a step back, stopping when it became clear that he was in danger of stepping off the road entirely, and watched as Zib waved her arms like she was trying to flag down a small plane. She had stopped walking to wave, and the others stopped as well, unwilling to leave her behind in this unfamiliar land.

So it was that all five of them were standing close together when the great white owl settled down behind them, folding its wings before they could brush against the ground. Jack and Soleil shied back. Niamh and Avery stayed precisely where they were, neither moving nor even seeming to particularly breathe.

Zib, however, cried, "Broom!" and flung herself at the owl, embracing it.

Here is another thing about birds in general, and owls in specific: while they can seem, and even be, quite large, much of their size is air. Their feathers catch and keep it, helping them to fly, and in most birds, those feathers don't lie flat against the body. When Zib wrapped her arms around the great white owl, she pressed his feathers down, and so for a moment, it looked like his body was swallowing her, enveloping the girl in a layer of marshmallow fluff.

Broom laughed—an odd sound, coming from an owl—and unfolded one wing, wrapping it gingerly around Zib's shoulders. "I do need to breathe, little friend," he said, and if the laughter had been odd, the speech was stranger still.

Zib made a small sound of dismay and let him go, stepping back but not quite away. "Broom, you're here!" she said needlessly. Then her face fell. "But we haven't found the Queen of Wands yet. We still can't save the Impossible City."

"The Queen is in her parlor, the light is in the tower," said Soleil, voice slow and wondering. She frowned as she looked from Jack to Niamh, silently asking them for answers that neither had to offer her. "And all is right with the world."

"All is *not* right with the world," said Broom. "They sent me because I am the Great Owl of the Air, and I felt it both when you entered and when you left the Kingdom that calls me. Oak and Meadowsweet are still back in the Kingdom of Coins, waiting for me to return to them."

"Three owls," said Avery slowly.

"Yes?"

"Only Soleil just finished explaining how there are four elements that make up absolutely everything in the Up-and-Under, and they match to the four Kings and Queens we've been running from or searching for." He fixed the great owl with an unwavering eye. "Why aren't there four of you?"

"There used to be," said Broom, and his impossible voice was heavy with regret. "Before the Queen of Wands disappeared, the Great Owl of Fire was known as Fern. She could be seen soaring through the smoke when the volcanos of Fire belched forth their ashes into the air, and she and I danced together often. But she vanished when the Queen did, and we have not seen her since."

"Is she dead?" asked Jack.

"None of us has found a body, nor has a fledgling come to wear her colors," said Oak. "Great Owls are not immortal. We die like anything else in the Up-and-Under, only when we do, a new Great Owl is hatched, to keep the balance of things. No such owl has hatched in the Kingdom of Fire. Fern still lives, somewhere."

"She isn't in the Kingdom of Air," said Jack— the first words he had spoken in the owl's presence. Shakily, he stepped forward and sank down until he was on one knee on the improbable road, head bowed, as if he were awaiting judgment or knight-hood. "Master Broom."

"Jack Daw," replied the owl, sounding halfway amused. "I have always known you, son of Air, even if we were never once allowed to meet. You do not bow to me. I am not your master."

Jack rose, still looking shaky. "But you are the custodian of my mother's element," he said. "With-out you, the Air would not answer, would not obey."

"Perhaps," said Broom. "But then, your mother saw to it that you were exiled in part from your birth-right before I could know you properly, and so while you remain of Air, you are not mine, and you do not bow to me." His massive head swiveled around, focusing on Avery and Zib. "As to the Queen of Wands, I know you haven't found her yet. The light is not in the tower. The tower has gone dark as dusk. Whoever was pretending that the Queen was home and all was well has abandoned their masquerade. Perhaps, with you children running about the Up-and-Under searching for the Queen, they no longer saw the point in pretense."

"What does that mean?" asked Avery.

"It means an army is rising in the Kingdom of Coins," said Broom, voice dark. "Even Oak, the Great Owl of Earth, can't find who calls them, or why. The King denies any knowledge of their point or purpose. We think he lies—the monarchs always lie—but we have no proof, and no authority in his Court. Soon, they will march on the City. The Impossible City will fall if you don't find her soon."

"We've reached the Kingdom of Fire!" cried Zib. "We've come so far and gone through so much! Surely that means we'll find the Queen!"

Broom spread his wings wide as a snowy horizon, and for a moment, all was dazzling white. "This is not a story to be solved," he said. "You don't earn success through suffering. What you earn with a step taken is the strength to take another step. You may yet fail. You may not find her. I came to tell you time is growing short, not to promise you success that isn't mine to give. Be quick, children, be quick and be careful, and remember, the clock is counting down, and the one who used to wind it is gone. When the time runs out, no more will be forthcoming."

With that, he launched himself back into the air, soaring silently away and leaving the five staring after him, each feeling even more lost than they had before his arrival. Soleil made a strange hiccupping sound. Zib turned to face her and saw that she was crying, fat tears rolling down her cheeks and dripping from her chin, only to evaporate with a sizzle when they struck the ground.

"Oh!" cried Zib. "Oh, Soleil, don't cry! I think we must be friends after all, for I want nothing more in all the world than for you not to cry!" She moved to the other girl's side, anxious. Had she been home, her mother would have offered her a handkerchief and a bracing cup of tea. Here, in the wild wastes of the Up-and-Under, she had neither thing to give. She had only comfort.

So comfort was what she would supply. "You haven't done anything wrong," she continued. "You weren't with us when we agreed to come searching for the Queen, not really, and you said you didn't remember everything the Crow Girl knew. It's not fair that she agreed and you have to follow through with what she said she'd do. It isn't fair at all."

"It's always like that, though," said Jack. "When

you say you'll do something, unless you plan to do it immediately and without hesitation, you're agreeing on behalf of someone who doesn't exist yet, someone you're eventually going to become. I'm not here because *I* choose to be. I'm here because the boy I was a day ago thought it was a good idea to defy his mother, and now this is the only way forward I have. So I keep choosing to keep going, and the me who isn't yet keeps on paying for it."

Zib blinked at him. It was Avery, however, who stepped in, saying, "But the you that you are and the you that you were are basically the same person. For Soleil, she was someone else altogether when she said that she would come with us."

Soleil was still crying, but her tears had started to slow. By the time she turned to Zib again, her eyes were dry. "I was crying because the Queen of Wands is never supposed to leave the Impossible City," she said. "Something has gone terribly, terribly wrong if she has. You're looking for her?"

"We are," said Niamh. "I can't enter the City as I am—drowned girls are too possible a thing to be allowed—but if we find the Queen, I'll be the first drowned girl to be a hero of the dry world, and the gates should open for me. We're all impossible things here. A drowned girl who wants to be a hero, two children from another world, a boy who's not a

Prince, not a Page, and not a monster, all at the same time, and now you, whatever you are. Can you still break into birds?"

"No," said Soleil. "I have a heart where a heart is supposed to be, and it knows how to be all one thing, but it doesn't know how to fly away."

"Then you're very possible," said Niamh, disappointed. "Well, I'm sure there's something impossible about you, and we'll find it yet."

Avery frowned. Jack Daw looked to him, slightly feathery eyebrows raised in question. "Yes?" he asked. "Is there something wrong with seeking a person's impossibility, to grant them access to the Impossible City?"

"Yes," said Avery firmly. "There's something wrong with acting like a person can ever be impossible. People are possible. We exist, that means we *must* be possible! It's . . . rude, and cruel, and wrong, to act like we're not!"

"But if all people are possible, then there can be no people in the City, and you can lock the gates and walk away."

Avery frowned again, deeper this time. "A City can't decide whether or not to let someone in!"

"Where you come from, maybe. Can a road decide who is or isn't allowed to walk on it, or where it wants to go?"

"No! That would be silly. Roads—whoa!" Avery pinwheeled his arms as the improbable road shifted beneath his feet, not disappearing as it had done when they walked across the Saltwise Sea, but reorienting itself just enough to serve as a reminder that it *could* vanish if it wanted to. All of them stumbled, except for Jack Daw, whose feet remained planted as firmly as they had ever been.

Zib, who had been leaning over to look at the strange white flowers, reasoning that they might dry Soleil's tears if only she could get to them, stumbled and fell, plummeting face-first onto the blackened landscape. She cried out as she fell, and Jack whipped around, his eyes going wide as he saw her go down. He lunged but was too slow to catch her. Avery was closer and slower to react, turning to see her fall and stumbling back, more firmly onto the road, as he covered his mouth with his hands.

"I'm sorry!" he cried, voice muffled by his fingers. "I'm sorry, I'm sorry, I didn't mean for anything to happen! I didn't realize—"

"You should have," said Niamh, not moving to help Jack and Zib. The water dripping from her body had begun to steam even before it hit the ground, and it was reasonably clear that she was nearing her boiling point. However much she may have wanted to help, she couldn't, not without risking her own life. "This is the *improbable road*. This isn't the first time it's reacted poorly to being treated like a common conveyance. We're lucky it didn't leave us altogether!"

"Zib? Zib, talk to me?" Jack grabbed Zib's leg where it still lay on the road, trying to pull her toward him without scraping her too harshly against the uneven ground. He succeeded in shifting her enough to reach out and fist his hands in the base of her sweater, reeling her into a seated position like a fisherman reels in a large catch, one inch at a time, moving as fast as he dared.

Zib remained limp, head dangling, face lost in the cloud of her own hair. Her hair wasn't on fire, which Jack tried to take as a good sign. He gathered her into his arms, rolling her over, so that her unburnt face was pointing toward the sky. Avery and Soleil crowded close, while Niamh stayed where she was, at the very center of the road, as far from danger as she could be without leaving them entirely. Even in the terror of the moment, none of them blamed her. She was too truly of water: they all knew that the heat was harming her, even if none of them knew for sure what would happen if she touched the fire.

"Zib?" Jack shook her, very slightly, searching her face for signs of damage.

There was none. She had fallen straight onto the hot and steaming ground, which none of them could stand to touch, and yet there were no scorch marks on her face, no signs of char on her clothes. Her eyes were closed. She was breathing, but if not for that, he might have thought that she had died on contact with the Kingdom of Fire.

Jack raised his head, looking from Soleil to Avery, and finally to Niamh. "She won't wake up," he said.

"When first I drowned, I didn't wake for weeks," said Niamh. "I was too much of water to understand myself, and so I slept, and healed, and learned who I was meant to be while I was safe in the arms of my new family."

"Zib didn't *drown*," said Avery.

"Zib touched the ground in a Kingdom without a Queen, and she never named her element," said Soleil. "If she was too much of fire, she may have been claimed, as Niamh was once, when she fell into the water and sank like a stone. There are drowned girls of every kind, in every Kingdom of the Up-and-Under. We may have lost Zib to one of those terrible truths."

"She's not a burning girl, though," said Jack, half frantically. "She's not on fire!"

Avery had never considered that drowned girls could be a phenomenon outside of the water, or that someone who came from the other side of the Forest of Boundaries could become one, regardless of the elements in play. "I told you, it doesn't work that way for people from our world," he said hotly.

"You've eaten food and drunk drinks from *this*

world," said Niamh. "You've made bargains and bartered things that can't be bartered in the world you came from, and you're not the first to come here. Not everyone who enters the Up-and-Under is so quick to seek the Impossible City and demand safe passage home. Not everyone *wants* to go home, and we don't force anyone to leave. How could we? Leaving the Up-and-Under is a thing you quest and fight for, not a thing that just happens. And the longer you stay here, the more this *is* your world. Your body has built pieces of itself out of things it found here. Your memories are filled with shadows of our story. You may be *from* somewhere else, but that doesn't mean that *here* has no power to transform you. You know better."

Avery looked away, a feeling of strange shame settling over him, as Jack gathered Zib into his arms and stood, lifting her away from the road. She hung limp against him, head lolling, not opening her eyes.

"If she were burning, she would be on fire," Jack said. "I think, whatever intent this Kingdom carries for her, it isn't ignition."

Jack looked down at the road then, and with all the cold imperiousness of someone who had been born a Queen's son, even if he had never been allowed to become a Prince, he said, "Take us to the Palace."

The road trembled again, but less fiercely this

time, quivering like a kitten on the verge of waking. Soleil sighed with apparent surprise, and the rest of them turned to see that the road, which had been stretching straight and true across the fields, now bent to the left ahead of where they stood, heading toward the distant, looming shape of a mountain so black that it sparkled in the smoky sunlight, like a chunk of onyx or obsidian dropped into the landscape.

Hoisting Zib higher in his arms, Jack began to walk, and the others followed.

SIX

INTO THE PALACE OF WANDS

More and more of the strange white flowers appeared around them as they walked, growing in larger and larger patches, until they were growing right up along the edges of the road, which seemed to have settled into the landscape until it had always been there and always *would* be there, a spoke in the great wheel of the Up-and-Under, unable to shift without disrupting the balance of everything. The small group continued to walk in a cluster, Zib hanging motionless in Jack's arms, her arms and legs swaying with every step he took.

She was still breathing, and they all took heart at that, even if she wasn't moving or responding when

they called her name. As long as she was breathing, there was still hope.

The more flowers pressed up against the edge of the road, the more the heat receded, until they were walking in what felt like a balmy spring day, and not a sweltering summer afternoon. The water dripping from Niamh was no longer steaming, and the tracks she left behind actually lingered for more than a few seconds. The color—never very pronounced, as she was dead and drowned and carried the cold pallor of the sea in her skin—was returning to her cheeks, and she looked altogether better than she had before the road turned.

Her improvement was reflected in Soleil's decline. As they drew closer to the black cliff, the older girl wilted, her shoulders drooping and her steps becoming less and less eager. She was almost shuffling by the time the shadow of the mountain fell over them, as gray as the smoke that swirled overhead. Flakes of ash covered the improbable road, and their feet left crisp prints behind them, all save for Niamh, whose steps made a sort of strange volcanic mud which dried as soon as she had moved along.

"How are we supposed to get up that?" asked Avery, practical as ever.

"The road is taking us to the Palace," said Soleil, with a certain resigned serenity. She sounded like she had given up completely and was hanging all her hopes on whatever they wound find when their trek was over and done. "All we have to do is follow the road, and it will get us there."

Avery, who had walked on this same road across the sea and across the sky, still looked dubious at the thought of following it up the side of a glittering black mountain. Then he glanced at Zib, whom he'd never known to be still but who now dangled limply in Jack's arms, and the doubt fled his face. He turned back to the mountain with renewed determination, and the group walked on.

The perfume of the little white flowers was beginning to overwhelm the hot-metal scent of the char that radiated from the earth around them. It was sweet and subtle, caught somewhere between corn-silk and roses, and Avery thought that if someone could capture that scent and make a perfume from it, they might find themselves rich beyond all measure. It occurred to him, rather suddenly, that outside of the Kingdom of Coins, he hadn't seen anyone in the Up-and-Under using money of any sort.

It may seem odd to us, who live in a world very different from the Up-and-Under, that Avery could have gone so very long without noticing the absence of money, but we must recall that as of the start of this story, Avery was a child. A relatively sheltered child, at that, who had never once asked himself the price of milk or eggs or bread. Those were things that were always simply there, provided by his parents. Not all children have this luxury. Too many must learn, very early, that things have costs, and sometimes there is not sufficient coin to match those costs. For them, money is a constant presence, part of every quest and conversation. For Avery, who had been given the great gift of comfortable ignorance, money was a thing given by grandparents on birthdays, transmutable into desired toys or tokens, but not the stuff of life.

The improbable road reached the base of the mountain and began to snake gently upward, following the curves and dips of a natural pathway worn into the stone. The group continued to walk along it, allowing the road to lure them up and away from the ground. They had gone perhaps twenty feet up the side of the mountain when Soleil made a small sound of discontent.

Jack turned to look at her. "What is it?" he asked.

Wordlessly, she pointed to the ground beneath their feet. Jack looked down.

The path they walked along was glittering black stone. The improbable road, fickle as ever, was gone, and they walked now without its iridescent guide to see that they reached the right destination.

Unlike Soleil, who remembered so little of the world that she might as well have been a stranger like

Avery or Zib, or Niamh, who came from a place so deeply drowned that she had never had purposeful need of the improbable road, Jack had been raised to respect and revere the road, which was the only true connection between the Kingdoms that could be assessed by those too common to carry a crown. The Kings and Queens could go where they liked, as could their Pages and consorts; the Great Owls were all but a law unto themselves. For everyone else, there was the road and only the road, and all else might as well have been stories and lies.

To see the road desert them now sent a shiver of cold slithering down his spine to wrap around his stomach, tight and constrictive as a hungry serpent. Jack swallowed and kept walking. Zib was not yet heavy in his arms, and the Palace of the Queen of Wands was as yet up ahead, still unseen. If the road had left them, either it disagreed with their destination, or it felt that they no longer needed its guidance.

Jack had no way of knowing one thing from the other, and so he continued onward, trusting the road not to have left them walking into danger. The improbable road had no true loyalties save to the Impossible City, which was its source and destination. They sought a place to care for Zib, yes, but they also sought the missing Queen of Wands at the request of the Great Owls themselves, and a way to access the Impossible City. Without the Queen, the City would fall to war, and the road would suffer as much as anyone else. He had to trust the road.

They all did.

Without the rainbow gleam to guide their steps, it was hard to see the pathway up the mountain, which was black on black and not very distinct from the rocks around it. Niamh, who had the sharpest eyes of the group, had to walk at the rear, in order to keep the water dripping from her skin from causing them to slip and fall. After perhaps another twenty feet, they came to an uneven halt, looking anxiously around as they sought the next step in their journey.

Avery was the first to hear the distant cellophane crackle of flames. He looked wildly around himself, seeking the source of the sound. Niamh, who was sensitive to the threat of fire, heard it second and looked back along the trail.

Jack heard the crackle and looked up, managing not to flinch as he met the gray-orange gaze of the Page of Gentle Embers.

The Page hovered in the air directly above the group, apparently buoyed upward by a heat shimmer in the air, which must have been as hot as an oven where it wrapped around the delicate figure of a child even younger than their congregation. Her eyes were the color of dying embers, and her hair was the radiant white-gold plume of a roaring bonfire. Her skin was more of a red shade, like a fire that was burning more gently but still consuming all it came into contact with. She wore nothing but a simple gray dress, its color mottled and streaked in a hundred shades of ash. Like Niamh, and frequently Zib, her feet were bare, and her toes dripped sparks the way Niamh's dripped water.

"Hello," said Jack, sounding slightly strangled.

"Hello," she replied, and her voice was at once the gentle crackle of a fireplace and the wild roar of an all-consuming forest fire. She turned in the air, until she was hanging quite upside-down as she studied them. "Shattered Prince of Air, drowned girl, and strangers. Who are you, and why do you approach the Palace of my Lady?"

"You know me," said Jack, voice not quite relaxing into its usual ease. "We've flown together, you and I."

"Yes," said the Page. "Flashfires can tear even through the Kingdom of Air, when the time calls for it, and your mother the Queen has never been foolish enough to try to deny me my playtime. But who are these with you?"

"Niamh, of the Frozen City," said Niamh. Her own voice only shook a little, even as she stood before a creature who could dehydrate her with the wave of a hand. In that moment, she was the bravest drowned girl to ever walk the Up-and-Under, and of her companions, none of them truly understood how bold she was being to answer at all.

"Soleil, of somewhere," said Soleil next. The Page fixed her with a curious eye, and she shrugged, shoulders rising and falling in a resigned motion. "I don't remember precisely where."

"You wear a gown of feathers," said the Page.

"My mother had her heart and her name for quite some time," said Jack. "She was a Crow Girl, with all that entails, stripped down to Air and emptiness. She's only had her heart and name to hand for a short while, and is still recovering."

"So she wears the gown because she has nothing else?" asked the Page.

Jack nodded, and she shifted her eyes to Avery, mystery solved and thus dismissed entirely. He squirmed, discomfort written in every line of his body. She flipped over in the air once more, so that she was regarding him right-side-up, rather than upside-down, and cocked her head, waiting for him to answer her half-forgotten question.

Avery swallowed. Avery looked down at his scuffed and shineless shoes. He looked up again, and said, in a soft voice, "Avery, of America."

"America?" The Page spun in her surprise, sending tiny sparks flying off into the air around her and stopping when she was quite upside-down. "I haven't met someone from America in the very longest of times! I'm sure I did, once before, but that was miles and miles and tales and tales ago, and wherever they've gone to, they didn't take me with them."

"Could they have?" asked Jack. "This is Zib, also of America." He hoisted her limp body a little higher, putting her on display. "We seek the Palace because she tripped, and fell, and struck the ground, and now she won't wake up."

"Oh." The Page drifted lower, rotating until she was all but upright again, her toes dangling only a few inches above the ground. The heat shimmer bearing her up was more apparent now, like a gauzy web keeping her suspended in the air. "Is she hurt?"

"She didn't bleed, and she doesn't seem to have any bruises," said Jack. "She didn't hit the ground that hard. I can't imagine why it would have hurt her so badly that she can't wake up now, but she's been like this since she fell. We need to get her somewhere safe, somewhere the fires are banked below burning, somewhere that people not made entirely of flame can breathe."

"The Palace," said the Page, as if she were introducing an entirely new idea and not parroting back the place Jack had already stated they were going. Some people are like that, very inclined to think that everything they say is fresh and original, and not at all based on anything that's come before. Most such people are arrogant. From the Page's tone, she wasn't arrogant, but simply one of those who has trouble remembering in the now what happened ten minutes ago. Like fire, she was a fickle creature. It was as she had been created to be.

"Yes," said Jack, keeping his own voice level and calm.

"You should take her there," said the Page, and shot straight up into the air, until she was about ten feet up the ground. "Follow me."

She began to fly off, not straight up the side of the mountain, but in a slow, looping pattern, and as the others followed below her, they found that she was tracing the pathway up the mountainside. It was still black-on-black, all but invisible in the shadows cast by the clouds overhead, but with her to guide them, they could walk it without fear of falling. Slowly, step by step, they made their way up the side of the mountain.

When they came to the end of the path, it was not to find themselves on the mountain's peak, or perhaps it was only that their definition of "peak" was incorrect, for they were at the top of the mountain, standing on a lip of stone no wider across than Soleil was tall, with the sheer fall back to the plains on one side, and a second, even more terrifying drop into a cauldron filled with bubbling lava on the other. A strut of stone jutted from the center of the roiling volcano, and atop it stood the Palace.

Unlike everything else they had seen in this place, it was neither charred nor ashen. It gleamed like a spire of rainbow crystal in the light that filtered through the clouds, at once transparent and every color the world had to offer. It had been carved into the rough shape of something Avery could recognize as a castle, but it was still rough and jagged around the edges, looking more grown than made, like it had simply chosen to take on a form they could identify with a seat of power.

A narrow bridge led across the lava to the palace doors. Avery and Niamh both eyed it with worry, for their own, if similar, reasons. Jack, however, stepped onto it without hesitation, walking straight toward the doors with Zib still dangling in his arms. Soleil followed close behind him, stepping lightly, seemingly unbothered by the potential fall into the volcano. The Page flitted back and forth between the two groups, still leaving sparks in her wake.

"The path you followed up the mountainside was narrower, and you didn't fall," she said, flipping upside-down again as she addressed Avery. "Why do you fear falling here?"

"Because that's lava," said Avery. The Page looked politely puzzled. Avery frowned. "People from America die if we fall into lava."

"Then you go to the Impossible City via the

graveyard path," said the Page. "Someone always does. Your drowned girl did, once."

Avery glanced to Niamh, who nodded.

"I told you I had been to the City, before I became too possible to tolerate," she said. "The graveyard path is always open to the dead, when we make our first journey. It's impossible for a dead person to make a trip on their own, until they find the graveyard path. That makes it possible for them, and the contradiction will get them past the gates. Once. Only once."

"That's not fair," protested Avery.

Niamh looked at him with tired, level eyes. "Child, when did anyone tell you that the Up-and-Under would be *fair*? Water doesn't care for fair or unfair when it drowns you. It only desires to drown."

"Fire is much the same," said the Page. "Fire only wants to burn. As long as our Queen of Wands keeps her light in the tower and claims the crown, the fires of the Up-and-Under will be kind when we can, will turn away from farms and houses, try not to pursue those who stumble into our infernos, but that's fire *here*, where it answers to a superior authority. Fire in your world simply swallows. It would eat everything there is, if only it could find a way."

Avery swallowed. "This doesn't make me trust the bridge," he said.

"The bridge is not made of fire," said the Page. "Not anymore, at least. When this Kingdom was shaped, it burned for *years*. Such fires as you have never once seen. Stone melted and gave way, sand became glass, wood was wiped from the land. The bridge *knows* fire, for it came from stone that survived that burning, but it is not burning now. It won't dissolve beneath your feet, and this is not the Kingdom of Wind. No playful breezes will rise to push you from your place. Not without my permission, and I have no intention of granting it, Avery from America."

Avery and Niamh exchanged an anxious look before stepping, in careful unison, onto the bridge.

As the Page had promised, it was sturdy stone, and they walked across it without incident to where the others waited, the Page soaring circles around them like some sort of strange bird circling a bicycle as it traveled down the road. When the five of them were once more united before the closed Palace doors, the Page looked to Jack.

"We would like to go *inside* the Palace," he said patiently.

"Oh! Well, why didn't you say so?" She shot upward in a shower of sparks, vanishing into the high spires of the Palace.

Jack, watching her go, smiled fondly and shook his

head before turning to the others, all of whom were watching him with varying degrees of confusion.

"Of the Pages, the Page of Gentle Embers is perhaps the kindest," he said. "The Page of Frozen Water is cruel for the sake of cruelty itself. The Page of Ceaseless Storms is cruel mostly because it pleases my mother, but he's cruel all the same. The Page of Sleeping Riches rarely chooses cruelty, because it's not profitable. But the Page of Gentle Embers is forever out and about, wherever there is Fire. She chooses kindness as much as she can, to please her Queen. Kindness is not a natural state of Fire. Remembering to be kind occupies much of her mind, and she can forget other things, however simple and straightforward they might seem to people who aren't working quite so constantly to refrain from setting everyone around them on fire."

"Oh," said Avery. "And that's why she thought we'd want to come here, but not want to come inside?"

"That, and she tends to be very literal," said Jack. "We didn't *say* we wanted to be inside the Palace."

The great door before them clicked before swinging slowly open, unlocked and pushed from the inside. The cluster of children took a step back, still well clear of the lava, to let it pass them. The room on the other side was a sea of shadows, and smelled faintly of char.

"We'll be safe in the Palace," said Jack, almost as if he was trying to convince himself, and carried Zib over the threshold into the shadowed room beyond.

The others, lacking any other choice, followed, and when Niamh stepped through, the door slammed shut behind her with an ominous crash.

SEVEN

ASHES AND EMBERS

The tall windows rimming the room were smeared with soot and ash, and the light that filtered through them was barely deserving of the name. The children could see each other, and could see their surroundings if they squinted very hard, but not the walls, or where most of the furniture had been placed. The pieces they *could* see were as stained with smoke as everything else around them, not draped with white sheets to protect them from neglect.

There is a certain texture that air acquires when it has been sitting undisturbed for a long while. You may have felt it when entering a sealed-off room of your home, or a place that had been abandoned. It is a

feeling of stillness so profound that it transforms the world around it, until every motion is a crime against the status quo. The air is very rarely still in its own Kingdom, and perhaps that was why Jack seemed quite so unsettled, and why his feathery hair seemed to puff itself out, just a little, like the feathers of a distressed bird.

The others had no such issues. Even Soleil walked forward, putting herself in front of Jack as she tilted her head back and gazed upward at the distant, oc-cluded ceiling. The shadows were too deep for her to see even a sliver of it; the room might as well have continued on forever. Still, she looked, and the others clustered around her, waiting for her to say something.

Niamh, who would never have thought herself likely to miss the Crow Girl, watched Soleil, while Jack and Avery both cast their eyes upward, into the gloom.

Finally, Soleil spoke.

"It seems . . . odd, that the Palace should be so deserted," she said. "The Queen of Wands is very often away, keeping her place in the Impossible City, keeping the light on in the tower, but she keeps a Court, unlike the Queen of Swords, who fears her own people too much to allow any save the winds and birds to attend on her. There should be people, even in the absence of the Queen. There should be light, and light, and the laughter of the unafraid. Not this dark and dusty silence."

"They started to wink out after the Queen disappeared," said a voice. They turned. There, approaching out of the shadows, was the Page. Her feet were planted firmly on the floor, and while her body gave off a faint, burning glow, she was less bright than she had been.

"It happened first and fastest to those who stayed with the Palace," she said. "Fern said it was because the Kingdom of Fire was out of balance. Without a Queen, it wanted to seek a new ruler, but it couldn't, because she wasn't dead or deposed, just missing. Fern went to look for her, and never flew back. And one by one, the courtiers and the petitioners disappeared. Like someone was extinguishing their candles."

There was a deep, immutable sorrow in her tone, like she couldn't imagine anything worse happening to anyone, ever.

"And the rest of the Kingdom?" asked Jack.

"First and fastest in the Palace, but second and slow everywhere else," said the Page. "I'm not the last denizen of the Kingdom, but I may as well be. The salamanders and pyrallis may still be out there, hiding in their homes and holes. I haven't gone to seek them out." She scuffed her toe against the ground. "They wouldn't welcome me, or they wouldn't have left me."

"People do many things when they're frightened," said Jack. He looked around the dim room again, seeing a little more clearly in the faint light cast by the Page. "Is there any way for you to turn the lights on? We may be safe here, but Zib still isn't waking up, and I need to set her down so we can examine her."

"Lights?"

"Most of us can't see in the dark," said Jack, with exquisite politeness.

Niamh, who should have been able to see in the dark, coming as she did from a place of drowned and infinite darkness, said nothing, only lifted her chin a little and held her tongue. More than any of them, she was an interloper in this land of flame and fury. If she brought its wrath down upon herself with a careless word, there was every chance that she might not survive.

But would any of them survive an inferno?

The Page stomped her foot against the floor, shedding sparks into the dark. Then she stomped again, clapping her hands at the same time, and the great chandelier overhead burst into sudden light. It was a massive thing, made of gleaming titanium and hung with teardrop diamonds. Its arms twisted and snaked together like the boughs of a tree, dripping with candles. Their flames cast dazzling rainbows through their diamond neighbors, until the whole room was alive with sparkling brilliance. Avery and Jack looked away, unable to bear looking directly into it for very long. Niamh had not tried to look in the first place.

Only Soleil continued to stare, her eyes wide and filled with wonder as much as with light.

Revealed, the room was massive, clearly as large as the receiving room in the Palace of Air, with a pair of winding staircases extending from the room opposite the entry, and wide, circular doors to either side, allowing the curious or the official to move deeper into the Palace.

And over everything lay a thick layer of char, radiating out from a point at the center of the floor. Jack looked at it, raising an eyebrow in silent question, and then at the Page, who shrugged.

"I'm a Page," she said. "I don't wink out. I'm not a candle. I'm a furnace. So when I felt the Kingdom trying to shift around me in such a way as to extinguish me entirely, I refused, and for a moment, I *blazed* the way I did before our Lady caught and tamed me. It stole all the air out of the room, I'm afraid. It rendered everything bright and burning. And when the flames died down, there was no one left but me. So I left."

"That makes sense," said Jack, looking around again until he spotted a low reclining couch, probably intended for the ladies of the Court when they felt the need to pause and take a rest. He carried Zib over to it, bending to carefully lower her to the ash-covered fabric. She sank down into it, eyes still closed, and as he pulled his arms away, he thought he heard her sigh. It was a small sound. If it wasn't his imagination, it was the first sound she had made since she fell.

Straightening, he turned back to face the Page. Avery was approaching her, his hands balled into fists by his sides, and Jack paused to watch.

It can be easy, when viewing the actions of one such as Jack Daw, or before him the Crow Girl, and assume they must think or feel as humans do: that Jack helped Zib out of fellow-feeling and affectionate regard, not out of some ancient, avian instinct. But instinct made up much of their motivation in their lives, and so seeing someone else draw the attention of the larger predator, Jack was content to remain as he was and allow Avery to take the risk.

"Why won't Zib wake up?" Avery asked.

The Page cocked her head, looking at him as if he were something new in her environment, something which had only just appeared in front of her without preamble or reason. "Oh, hello, Avery from America," she said, after a silence that was slightly too long to be comfortable. "Zib?"

Frustrated, Avery gestured to Zib, sprawled motionless on the ashy couch. Niamh, seeing his discomfort, began to start forward, as if to intervene, only for the fear of fire to stop her. She, like Jack, could only act according to her nature. That is the true weakness of elemental things, you see: they might represent an element, or a season, or an idea, which gives them great control and command over the forces they embody. But when they are called upon to act against their own natures, they will find themselves frozen, unable to push forward. A human, however—a true human is all the elements together, and a thousand thousand elements not so recklessly embodied! Each human has their own individual nature, and can act according to their own individual needs.

Avery knew that the Page might burn him. But unlike Niamh, who feared evaporation, he feared being burnt in the abstract way of a child who had yet to press his hand against the surface of a hot stove. It was a known danger, certainly, while still remaining an unexplored land. Unexplored lands will always carry temptation to the young, who must wonder what mysteries they could find if they were only allowed to go there. In this case, the land Avery approached contained only the possibility of pain, but he didn't know that, not yet. He only knew that he was concerned for his friend, and wanted to help her as he could.

"The extinguished girl?" asked the Page, still in the same tone of vague curiosity that she had brought to repeating Zib's name.

"She's not *extinguished*; she was never on fire," said Avery. "She's asleep. Why won't she wake up?"

"Oh, but she is," said the Page. "She's still here because she's not entirely made of fire, but so much of her is that when she touched the ground, whatever's been blowing out the citizens whisked her away as well. She's bound to be wherever they are."

Oddly enough, it was only when she speculated on where Zib—and by extension, the other denizens of the Kingdom of Fire—might have been that the curiosity sank out of her tone, replaced by puzzlement and disinterest.

Jack frowned, taking a half step toward her, as the part of him that was closest to human pushed instinct aside. "Do you know where that is?"

"In order for me to know, I'd have to have gone there and come back again, and wherever it is that they're all going off to, no one's come back." The Page pushed her lower lip out in a pronounced pout. "I wish they would. It's been awfully lonely since I left the Palace."

"Are all the other rooms burnt like this one?" asked Niamh. "Is there a safe place where we can sleep?"

"Only this one," said the Page. "I didn't flare up in all the rooms, just here."

"Jack? Is Zib still breathing?"

"She is," he confirmed.

Niamh nodded. "Then we sleep here and see if we can find something to fix for our supper, and in the morning, we go looking for wherever it is that the people of the Kingdom have been going to when they winked out. If part of Zib is there, maybe we can bring it back with us and wake her up."

It was an odd proposal. It was also the best idea any of them had had so far. It can be easy, when reading a story, especially if the story focuses entirely or in part on people older than ourselves, to think that they are so grown-up and mature, and so prepared for everything. But when we step back and truly look at the five of them—six, if we were to include the Page—we would see only five children of varying ages, as lost and confused as you or I would be in the same situation.

Like the Page, Niamh was older than she seemed, and while this Kingdom's element was not her own, she had some experience with elements whisking people away according to their own desires. One by one, the others nodded, even Jack, although he glanced back at Zib when he did so, honest regret in his eyes.

"Where are the bedrooms?" asked Niamh.

"Up the stairs," said the Page. "But the kitchens are through there." She pointed.

As if in answer to her gesture, Soleil's stomach made an audible sound of complaint. Jack laughed, startled into the sound, and stepped entirely away from the couch where Zib was sleeping.

"Food first," he said decisively.

The others nodded, and their course was set.

Through the door at the side of the room, they found a long stone-walled hallway. There was no paint or wallpaper, only bare, inflammable rock. Avery wrinkled his nose in faint disapproval but said nothing as they followed the Page past several closed doors to another wide half-circle doorway. On the other side was a vast, echoing kitchen, the walls lined with glassed-in sconces that burst into flame as soon as the Page stepped into the room, burning bright enough to illuminate everything around them.

Almost an entire wall was occupied by enormous open-faced ovens. Another was dominated by workstations, while the third held racks upon racks of food, fresh meat, fruits and vegetables, even bread, all of it looking as perfect as if it had just been prepared. Not a scrap of it appeared to be uncooked.

Avery shot the Page a curious glance.

"We eat ash and ember," she said with a shrug. "The chefs prepare everything and then freeze it so it won't get any older than it was when they finished it, and we throw it into the ovens and burn it to a perfect crisp when it's time for a banquet or a feast."

"Fire is always hungry." Soleil's voice was distant and dreamy, as if she were saying something she had only just remembered. "If the fuel for people made of Fire is the kind of food that other people eat, only charred and destroyed, it makes sense that they'd keep as much of it to hand as they could."

"How do they stop everything like this?" asked Niamh.

"Oh, that's a simple matter." The Page waved her hand, dismissing the question. "Our chefs ask very nicely, and Time obliges. Time is a form of Fire, after all."

Avery had never heard this before, and thought that it couldn't possibly be correct. Still, he didn't want to argue with the burning girl. Not when he could see a bowl of fresh bonberries on the shelf, their skins somehow, impossibly, gleaming with drops of fresh dew and vibrant with ripeness. He could almost taste their deliciousness.

Hunger is a natural predator. It follows and finds us all, and there's no stopping it for long. In a way, it's an element all of its own. Avery was tired and scared and sad, and halfway worried that he was being self-ish, because half his sadness was from the idea that without Zib, he wouldn't be able to enter the Impossible City, wouldn't be able to go home ever again.

A certain amount of selfishness is allowed on an adventure. It makes the dangers more surmount-able, makes the risks easier to understand. But Avery had been raised to believe that selfish was the worst thing he could be. Worrying about himself when Zib wouldn't wake up felt selfish and sour, and the fact that he was upset about how Zib's condition was making *him* feel only made things worse.

It was a terrible, seemingly unbreakable spiral leading down into a deep, dark place. Desperation not to strike the bottom led him to move toward the shelves and reach for the bowl of berries. There was a tingle as his hands passed the edge of the shelf, like he was reaching through a soap bubble. Then the feeling was gone. He lifted the bowl and pulled it to his chest, already munching as he turned back to the others. They moved to the shelves, selecting their own meals—all save the Page, who only stood and watched.

Avery blinked at her. "Aren't you hungry?" he asked.

"Starving," she said in a doleful tone.

"Then why don't you eat?"

"We all have our tasks, and mine isn't cooking," she said.

Avery blinked again. "I don't think my task is cooking either, but I can make spaghetti sauce and scrambled eggs and put a chicken in the oven to roast," he said. "Can you not cook anything at *all*?"

The Page looked at Jack. "Tell him how it works in the elemental Kingdoms, since it seems the rules are different in America," she said. "Tell him why I can't."

"Remember how the Page of Ceaseless Storms

watched and reported to my mother, and didn't do much else?" asked Jack. "Or how the carrying clouds carried people and the winds answered wishes, and nothing beyond that?"

"Wishes!" said Avery. "Niamh, you said we each got three of them. Zib used one of hers. I didn't use any of mine. Can we use them now?"

"If a wind was listening, and strong enough to carry things past the borders of the Kingdom of Air, it might be possible," said Niamh dubiously. "But it would mean catching the attention of a wind, and the attention of a wind might well come with the attention of the Queen. She's respecting the border right now, out of courtesy if nothing else. Catch her eye and she can decide to change that."

"Oh," said Avery, wilting a little. For just a moment, he'd seen a way to finish all of this and get himself home, with or without Zib by his side. "With" would be better, of course. "With" would mean he'd been a good person, and maybe even a hero. But "without" would still put him back in his own bed and seated at his own table, with his mother's pot roast in front of him. Maybe pot roast wouldn't really be nicer than bonberries, but a thing that's missed and mourned for will always seem sweeter than a thing that's close to hand.

"Better not to go wishing," said Jack.

"I guess."

One by one, they chose their dinners, all save the Page, who refused Avery's offer to char her a plate and only watched them with smoldering and sorrowful eyes. Then she led them out of the kitchen and back to the Palace, up the stairs to the rooms above, that they might sleep and face the coming day—the coming war—fresh and rested.

Jack carried Zib the whole way.

EIGHT
THE TOWER LOST

Morning came to the Kingdom of Fire as a nearly imperceptible change in the brightness outside the windows. The fires of the Kingdom had burned throughout the night, glowing red and gold and making true darkness impossible, save in sealed rooms such as the Palace contained. The fires continued to burn as the sun rose, and what sunlight reached the Palace did so after filtering through a thick layer of smoke and ash, becoming watered-down and almost absent by the time it struck the glass.

Still, it was enough to wake Avery, who had never been inclined to sleep particularly deeply. He sat up, for the first time taking proper stock of the room

where he'd spent the night. Unlike the Palace of Air, where the rooms had been generously appointed and seemingly tailored to their occupants, this room was plain and spare, with stone walls that had been brushed with a thin layer of white paint, more for appearances than anything else. The furniture was heavy, seemingly hewn from great trees and joined together through sheer force of conviction. Who needed nails or structure when piling four logs one atop another could be counted as a bed?

It was a comfortable bed, for all of that, plushly appointed with feather mattress, coverlet, and pillow. A feather had escaped one of the pillows. It glowed red and golden in the thin sunlight, seeming to burn from the inside. Avery picked it up, staring in wonder. Was everything here born from fire? The thought was a daunting one.

Feeling grimy and unsettled in the clothes he'd now been wearing, over and over, since arriving in the Up-and-Under, Avery slid out of the bed. There had been so many fine things to wear in the Kingdom of Air! But when they fled, they had stolen nothing but Soleil's heart and Jack Daw himself, and there was no going back now. What he had with him was what he would have until their journey brought them to the Impossible City, and onward to home.

He was going to hug his mother for a whole hour when he got back to her. He was going to sit with his father and tell the grave, thoughtful man who had raised him about all of his adventures, and how surely this meant he was grown enough now to be allowed to stay up until eight with the adults. As soon as he got home.

Rubbing sleep from his eyes, Avery walked to the window and looked out on the land. It spread out below the Palace in a scrimshaw map of black and red and ashen gray, dotted with patches of white that he thought must be more of those little flowers. If he looked one way, he could see the clear sky and high cliffs of the Kingdom of Air. If he looked the other, he could see the flat, inviting green fields of the Kingdom of Earth, and beyond them, the tall spires of the Impossible City itself. It seemed so close, from this height.

It seemed so incredibly far away. Avery turned away from the window and started for the door, pausing to retrieve his scuffed, shineless shoes from the floor as he went, on his way to find out wherever it was that Zib had gone. Another pointless digression from the real task at hand.

A pang of guilt followed the thought. Waking Zib wasn't pointless. It was essential. She had come with him through the Forest of Boundaries; she was as lost and out of place here as he was. If she had adapted more quickly to this place and its ridiculous rules, it was only because she was a more quick-tempered person, prone to fits of nonsense, immune to caution. She had as much of a right to go home as he did.

So no, this digression wasn't pointless. It was an obstacle on the way to the true goal, to finding and rescuing the Queen of Wands, wherever she had gone. Had anyone checked the tower they kept going on about? If she was supposed to be tending some sort of light there, perhaps that was where they would find her, striking matches that refused to catch and trying to relight some sort of complicated lamp.

He opened the door. Soleil was standing in the hall outside his room, her back up against the wall and a dreamy look in her eyes. He gasped, jerking backward in surprise. She slowly seemed to focus on his face, blinking twice. It was strange: before the first blink, she was a stranger, gazing off into something he couldn't see. After it, she was the Crow Girl, sharp, strange, and familiar. And after the second blink, she was Soleil, a little lost, a little wounded, and still new to him. To herself as well, in all the ways that counted.

"There you are," she said. "I was wondering when someone else would wake up. I thought Jack would be the first, since he's worried about Zib, but his door is still closed. Then I thought it might be Niamh, because she's too scared to sleep very well, but she hasn't been moving around at all. So I came down to wait here for you to get up."

"Did you sleep?"

Soleil cocked her head. "I don't know. I closed my eyes, and everything got fuzzy for a while, but how am I supposed to know if that meant I slept or not?"

"Did you dream?"

This time, she frowned. "I don't think dreaming is something I do anymore. Not since the Queen of Swords took my heart out. Crows don't dream, and I seem to have lost the knack while I was made of them."

"Oh." Avery paused. It seemed very sad, not to dream. But he wasn't sure that Soleil would want him feeling sorry for her, or would take it kindly if he said he did. So he forced a smile and said, "Maybe they'll come back, now that you're not made of crows anymore? You haven't been a girl again for very long. It might just take time."

"Maybe," she said, voice dubious.

"What can you tell me about the tower?"

"The tower?" she asked with some surprise.

"The one where the Queen of Wands is supposed to keep her light."

"Oh. The tower in the Impossible City." Soleil turned her vague expression toward the door to Avery's room. "May I come in?"

The room was a borrowed one. Odd as it felt to have a girl asking to come into what had been *his* room, however temporarily, Avery didn't have a good reason to tell her no. All the manners his parents had worked so hard to instill into him told him that he couldn't tell her yes, not without shaming them both, and so he didn't say anything at all, just stepped aside and let her interpret his gesture as she liked.

She stepped right past him without hesitating. Maybe the rules about boys and girls going into one another's rooms were different in the Up-and-Under. All the *other* rules were different here; why not that one? Not looking at his unmade bed or back in his direction, she made her way straight for the window, bracing her hands against the sill and leaning far, far out, past the point that should have been safe.

Suddenly anxious, Avery rushed to grab her arm and pull her back into the room. "You're not made of birds anymore," he said. "If you fall, you'll fall the whole way down."

"Or the improbable road will come back and catch me."

"Does it do that very often when people are falling?"

"Not ever that I've heard of," she said, and rolled her shoulders in an easy, unconcerned shrug. "But I don't think the road would let either one of us fall right now. I think . . . I think it wants us to make it to the Impossible City. I don't know why I think that. I just do."

"Well . . . please don't fall, okay? I don't want to

find out that you're wrong when you splash on the ground."

Soleil wrinkled her nose. "I wouldn't splash. Not unless I fell into lava, and even then I wouldn't splash much. Does the ground usually splash where you're from?"

"No, it— Never mind." Avery sighed. Why was everyone in this world so *frustrating*? This would have been so much easier if Zib were awake. She was better than he was at talking to the people who thought the way the Up-and-Under wanted them to think, who believed the way it wanted them to believe.

"You asked, though."

"Asked what?"

"To see the tower." Soleil shook him off her arm and leaned out the window again—not as far this time, not so far that his heart leapt into his throat and threatened to choke the life out of him. Raising her right arm, she pointed to a spot on the horizon. "See? There it is, right where it's always been."

Avery moved to follow the line of her finger, and almost gasped before he thought better of it and caught himself, going perfectly still. Really, he shouldn't have been surprised. They'd known all along where the Queen of Wands was meant to be. Where she was supposed and expected to be.

Soleil was pointing to the Impossible City. To the

highest spire on the tallest tower, a narrow needle of glass and stone that stabbed upward from the rest of the city skyline as if it were intended to spear the sun.

There was a single window there, very high up, visible only by the glint of sunlight against glass. Even that reflection felt like it shouldn't have been enough, like it shouldn't have been possible to pick out such a small detail at such a great distance. Ah, but this was the Up-and-Under. As it seemed determined to remind him, the rules were different here.

"That's the tower," she said. "It's attuned to whichever Kingdom currently holds the Crown. It's belonged to the Queen of Wands for as long as I can remember. Longer, probably, since I can't remember very long at all. She's supposed to climb the high stairs every night and light the lantern at the very top, so it can shine out and light up the whole Up-and-Under."

"But if she does that, how could she ever have disappeared without everyone knowing about it immediately?" asked Avery.

Soleil was quiet for a while, seeming to really consider the question. Finally, in a voice that dripped as slow as honey from a comb, she said, "If she . . . sometimes wanted to have a little space to herself, a chance to breathe without feeling the weight of the crown pressing her down, if she wanted to be as weightless as a flame is meant to be, as she had been before she claimed the City . . . if those were things she wanted for her own, she could very easily have asked a candle or cinder from her Court to make the journey for her on occasion. Candles and cinders are simple things. They give their loyalties and that's that: they're done. They never choose anyone else, and they never betray the ones they've promised themselves to. Embers and torches are more complicated. If she'd asked one of *them,* they might have been clever or complicated enough to betray her absence, to tell someone she wasn't there. But a candle or cinder who'd promised to keep lighting the torch while she was away, they'd just keep on doing it, always and forever, until someone else made them stop. Until . . ." Soleil paused then, pressing the fingers of one hand to her temple, and made a small sound of dismay. It was cousin to a crow's cry, deep and rough and almost inhuman, and it alarmed Avery down to his very core.

Once again he took her arm, as if to pull her back from some impossible precipice. He tugged her gently away from the window and led her to the bed, guiding her into a sitting position.

She didn't lower her hand until he stepped between her and the window, blocking even the idea of the Impossible City from view. Then she stopped, and blinked, and focused on him for the first time.

"The tower is the beacon that tells the Up-and-Under that all is well in the Impossible City," she said. "No one has to be afraid of anything but the ordinary dangers when the tower is lit. A bad bargain might leave you silenced, or a monarch might make you a monster, but nothing really *bad* can happen, not while the light is on. When the light is off . . ." She stopped, and shuddered.

"When the tower's not lit, the other Kings and Queens know that the City has no defenses," said Jack. Avery turned, somehow unsurprised to find Jack standing in the doorway to his room. Unlike Avery himself, and even Soleil, Jack was perfectly groomed and put together, with no indication that he'd just gotten out of bed, or that he'd been forced to go to sleep without a shower or brushing his teeth. "When the tower's not lit, anyone can take the City."

"They can't when there's a light on?"

"When there's a light on, the current ruler is in residence, and it's just not done." Jack shrugged. "No one makes war when it might inconvenience another element."

"That's ridiculous."

"Why? How do you make war in America?"

Avery opened his mouth, only to close it again when he realized he didn't know the answer. He knew what war *was*, of course—everyone knew what war *was*—but not how it happened, or why, or how it was declared. He supposed that sometimes people must be so angry with one another that they didn't see anything else that they could possibly do. He also supposed that if he had any way not to be in the middle of a war, he should make the choice that meant he wouldn't be there.

"So we wake Zib, we find the Queen, and we put the light back on," he said firmly. "Then there's not a war, and we can finally get into the Impossible City where she can send us home."

"You make it sound so easy," said Soleil. "Is everything easy in America?"

"Yes," said Avery, with the simple conviction of a child who had been protected and cared for all the days of his life, who had never been forced to confront the idea that maybe everything wasn't easy in America.

"We should all go there, then," said Jack. "When this is over. We should go with you when you go back, and see a world where everything is easy."

The thought of his strange and impossible companions in his orderly home, in front of his precise and polished parents, sent a shiver running down Avery's spine and slapped the conviction right out of him. He sat down next to Soleil on the bed, staring at the window. Only the barest edge of the Impossible City was visible from this angle, gleaming in the wan sunlight, as distant as a dream. Soleil was right. He made it sound so easy, and even if everything *was* easy in America, he wasn't in America now. He was in the Up-and-Under, where some things were easy when they shouldn't have been, and even more things were impossibly hard.

Tears suddenly prickled in the corners of his eyes. He blinked them back as fiercely as he knew how, trying to force them away. Avery had never believed in the idea that boys didn't cry—he was a boy, and cried, and that meant boys *must* cry sometimes, and no one got to say when sometimes was, so he could cry whenever he needed to. That didn't mean he wanted to sit here weeping when there was so much yet to be done.

A sizzling sound came from the hall outside the room. All three of them turned. Niamh and the Page were standing in the doorway, too close together to be comfortable for either one of them: the sizzling sound was the water that dripped from Niamh's skin boiling away to nothing before it struck the floor. From the look on the Page's face, whatever sensation accompanied this wasn't pleasant for her either.

"It's morning now, and you've all eaten and slept, and your friend is still asleep as anything," said the Page.

"We should go," said Niamh.

"How?" asked Avery. "The whole kingdom's burning all the time. Zib barely even *touched* the ground and she fell asleep and won't wake up! Without the improbable road, we can't go anywhere. We're trapped here."

"That's not quite so," said Soleil. "The road left

when we were only halfway up the mountain to the Palace. It got us going the right direction, and then it went off to do something else. The improbable road wouldn't put us in danger."

"Now I know you're not the Crow Girl anymore," said Avery. "The improbable road dropped us right smack in the middle of the Saltwise Sea. We almost drowned. We *would* have drowned, if a big sea monster hadn't come along and swallowed us all alive! Some of your crows weren't so lucky. You lost big parts of yourself when that happened—or she did, anyway."

"But the improbable road knew the Lady of Salt and Sorrow was watching out for us," said Niamh, moving away from the Page as she came all the way into the room. "It knew she would save us. Maybe she didn't save us fast enough, but the road couldn't know that. It's a road."

"Where I come from, roads don't know *anything*," said Avery. "Don't act like I should already know what a road does or doesn't understand!"

"Regardless," said Niamh. "We were walking on the soil of the Kingdom of Fire for quite some time, and none of us blew out like Zib did."

"The citizens blew out and didn't leave anything behind, because they were all the way fire," said the Page. "Your friend is *mostly* fire, so when the part of her that's made to burn vanished, there wasn't

95

enough left for the rest of her to keep moving around on its own. But she's still here because parts of her aren't fire."

"Aren't any of us mostly fire?" asked Avery.

The Page looked at him solemnly. "You're mostly earth. The drowned girl is mostly water. The bird boy is mostly air. And your fifth . . . her, I cannot read." Her eyes skated over Soleil before landing on the window, almost as if she couldn't stand to look directly at the older girl for too long. "What element she carries is between her and the Up-and-Under, and no concern of mine."

Avery frowned. Niamh and Jack walking their elements without being swallowed whole as Zib had been made a certain amount of sense to him, but if he was mostly earth, as people kept insisting, shouldn't he have lost consciousness as soon as he left the Forest of Boundaries for the Kingdom of Earth? The King of Coins should have taken him then.

Or maybe it was the presence of the King, whom they had never met, who now raised an army to march against the Impossible City, that had prevented him from being taken.

Jack, apparently following the tangle of Avery's thoughts from the expressions chasing one another across his face, snorted. "You came over the wall, yeah?"

When Avery nodded, so did he, one sharp, decisive jerk of his head.

"That's it, then," he said. Avery looked at him blankly. Jack sighed. "You came over the wall and through the Forest, straight into the Kingdom of Cups. But you had just come out of America. Your elements were still all jumbled up and mixed together. It's like . . . like going outside on a hot day when you've been in a nice, cool room for hours. Even if the ground *should* burn your feet, it doesn't at first. You can walk around for whole minutes before enough of the cold seeps out of you for the heat to start working its way in. Elements are the same way. If we could flip your whole journey around, so that you started here and came there last before the City, we'd probably flip around which one of you is awake and which isn't."

Avery blinked. It made sense when he looked at it like that. Which, of course, meant that he couldn't trust it, not really. If there was one thing he'd learned about the Up-and-Under, it was that if something seemed to make sense to him, that probably meant it didn't make sense at all when looked at from any sort of proper distance.

"Do you have any idea where the fire that's supposed to be in Zib would have gone when it left her?" asked Avery.

"No," said the Page. "If I did, I would have gone

looking a long time ago. I don't like being lonely. Pages aren't supposed to be lonely. We're always supposed to be right at the middle of the Court, so we can remember why we belong there, and not turn into natural disasters while nobody's keeping an eye on us."

Avery blinked.

Soleil stepped forward. "I don't know how much of what I think I know about this kingdom is accurate and how much is me halfway remembering things that the person I was for a little while knew but I don't. I just . . . isn't there a place called the Candle Grove? If we've lost a bunch of people you say winked out like candles, and there are people here in the Kingdom of Wands *called* candles, maybe they've gone to the Candle Grove?"

"It's possible," said the Page. "I don't know any reason why it wouldn't be possible."

"Candles don't go anywhere when you blow them out," said Avery crossly.

"Maybe not in America. But here in the Up-and-Under, anything that's made of a purified element can't be wiped out for real and proper. If the candles went out here, they lit somewhere else. The Candle Grove makes as much sense as anywhere else." She gave Soleil a sharp look. "But how do *you* know about that?"

Soleil looked uncomfortable, and didn't reply.

"It doesn't matter how she knows," said Jack. "If she's right and this place exists, that's good enough for me. How will we get there without burning ourselves? The road left us on the side of a melted glass mountain that had long since cooled and hardened. The rest of the Kingdom may well be more molten."

"There are special shoes in the dignitary's chambers," said the Page.

"Then we wear those," said Jack, the only one of them who could fly above the burning. The reason he intended to walk became apparent a sentence later: "I'll carry Zib."

If Jack was willing to commit himself to staying on the ground for however far they had to go, the rest of them had no excuse. Feeling suddenly small, Avery nodded and followed the Page back down the stairs to another room off the main arrival hall, this one small and sparse and lined with shelves. Each shelf was filled with shoeboxes. Not ordinary shoeboxes made of thin wood or thick corrugated cardboard, no: these boxes were made from sheets of hammered silver joined together at the corners with beads of shining solder. The shoes they contained were equally extraordinary.

Each pair was identical, save for size, slip-on, flat-soled, with no noticeable tread; they looked like they should have been slippery, like trying to walk on sheets of glass instead of proper shoes. They were made of some strong, flexible material that glimmered like golden starlight, not any single proper color but a cascade of every color possible, pink tumbling over yellow over green over silver. It was hard to look directly at them. Even Soleil looked briefly impressed before she found a pair in her own size and slipped them onto her previously bare feet.

One by one they found shoes that would suit them. Jack took the time to find a pair that would fit Zib, sliding them onto her feet with care before hoisting her into his arms and turning toward the Palace door. The Page matched him step for step, and the others fell in behind, seeing nothing else that could possibly be done at this stage of the story. They were no longer on the road, which was a straight line that seemed inevitable in its continual passage, but they were on a path all the same, following it straight and true to make it to the other side.

Out of the Palace they walked, and the doors slammed shut behind them, and they moved on, down the side of the mountain, with the Page beside them and no road to guide the way.

They walked into the ashy morning air, and the story rose up to meet them, for what else could the story do?

NINE

SUBJECTS OF THE STORY

But we are part of this story too, even if we do not act within it: observation changes all things. By watching these events unfold, we render them inevitable, impossible to avoid. Put the story down and walk away, and while it may continue on, it will do so without witness, and thus cannot be said to be truly told. We are in communication, you and I, children of the same phrase, tethered to the same pulse and pauses. We are kin.

So we follow them, five children and one creature of fire that *looks* like a child, speaks at times as a child, but is something else altogether. And who can say that three of the five are children as we understand

the idea of childhood? Niamh had drowned as an infant, and stopped her growing up, such as it was, in the instant she had been exiled from her watery grave. Jack had been born as human as anyone was in the Up-and-Under, but his heart had been stolen while he was still swaddled in his cradle, replaced by a clattering of jackdaws. He could be exactly as old as he appeared, or half as old—charting his growth against the curious calendar of corvids—or five times and more. Soleil, in addition to being the newest member of their company, was perhaps the least understood of all. Like Jack, she had spent her time as a subject of a different species, following a different set of rules. Unlike Jack, they had no evidence that she had been human in the beginning. Perhaps she was a line of music or a shaft of sunlight, somehow bound in physical form. With no way of knowing, there was no true way to guess her age.

Still, it is easier to call them children, and so children we shall call them as we describe their descent down the mountain to the burning plains, where the visible earth was still black riveted with red, as if the crust on the ground was on the verge of cracking open to release the flames beneath. The little white flowers had continued to spread during the night, blanketing everything: the blackened earth was a lacey spiderweb sketched between patches of flowers. Their perfume filled the air, heavy and indescribable.

Avery sniffed. "Peppermint and hot chocolate," he said in a wondering tone. "The flowers smell like . . . like Christmas morning?"

"Try again," suggested Niamh, stepping carefully to avoid stepping on either the white flowers or the red splits in the earth. It made her steps exaggerated, like she was tiptoeing into the first stages of some complicated dance.

Avery sniffed again. "Watermelon and cherry ice pops," he said, even more wondering, and even more confused. "Why . . . how . . . those things don't smell anything alike at all!"

"The fireflowers will always smell like whatever a person likes best in all the world," said the Page, once again floating a few feet in the air, drifting along beside them with no apparent effort. "So everyone smells them differently. There's something similar that grows in the Kingdom of Cups. Bonberries, I think they're called."

"Yes," said Avery. "I ate some in the kitchen. How do you not know what bonberries are, if you have them in the kitchen?"

"I wouldn't know what they *taste* like," she said, affronted. "Everything I eat is properly burned into ashes, and has no flavor but the fire."

Avery looked properly horrified. The idea of eating something that had been intentionally burnt until it had no flavor left but char was as alien to him as a fresh bonberry would have been to the Page of Gentle Embers. Fortunately for everyone, the Page was as fickle as the flame that fueled her, and rather than taking offense at his expression, she drifted away, moving to float in the air beside Jack and natter away at him about some point of politics between the lands of Fire and Air. Avery watched her go, almost glad he couldn't hear what she was saying. It would surely have been as horrifying as her ideas about food.

"What do the flowers smell like to you?" he asked, looking to Niamh.

She shrugged. "Deep, salty water, and kelp drying in the storerooms where our chefs keep bubbles of air to help them prepare our meals. You can't light a fire below the water, even in the sunken cities, and some foods taste better after they've been dried and rehydrated. I don't know why. I don't even know if the chefs know why. They just stumbled over it at some point in the deep past, and they keep doing it because it only takes deciding it's too much trouble once to be reminded why we bother."

"Oh," said Avery.

"I want to go home as badly as you do; never forget that," she said, looking straight ahead at the burning horizon. "My city may be denied to me until the ice above it thaws, but once I go home, the Lady of Salt and Sorrow can go home as well, and all can be set to right in the Up-and-Under."

"Oh," said Avery again, more softly, and turned his attention to Soleil.

She walked with slow, deliberate care, watching the ground to be sure she didn't step on any of the flowers. Unlike Niamh, she didn't seem to worry about stepping on the veins of red that ran through the black. They didn't spark or flare when she stepped on them, making Avery feel more secure in his own forward steps.

"What do the flowers smell like to you?" he asked.

Soleil inhaled, then paused, expression going quizzical as she tried to find an answer to his question. She breathed in again, more sharply. "Nothing," she said finally. "They don't smell like anything at all. I smell the ashes in the air, and the burning from the magma below us, but I don't smell any flowers."

"The Page said they smell like whatever a person likes best," said Avery. "Maybe you don't like anything yet, so you don't know what you like best?"

"I know I like you, and Zib, and Jack, and Niamh," said Soleil.

"Yeah, but none of us smell like anything nice.

Unless we haven't been bathing, we mostly don't smell like anything at all, and when we haven't washed, what we smell like isn't so pleasant." Avery wrinkled his nose at the thought. He might be too young yet to get really *smelly* like some of the boys from school, but he would be their age one day, and he didn't want to be. Not if it meant his socks would smell like something had died in them. The very thought offended him on a basic, material level.

"And I know I'm not supposed to eat people, so if the flowers smelled like you, or what I thought you smelled like, I'd never get to know for sure if I was right." Soleil looked briefly heartbroken, like this was somehow something terrible.

Avery considered walking faster to get away from her, if she was going to have that speculative what-would-you-taste-like look on her face. "Is eating people common here?" he asked.

"Mostly it's monsters that do it, and some of the smaller elementals, but I'm a people, and people don't usually eat each other," she said.

"That's good, then. Eating people isn't common where I come from, either."

"America, yes?" Avery nodded, and Soleil sighed. "And when we find the Queen of Wands, she'll open up the Impossible City for you and Zib, and you'll go back there, and maybe never come back here ever again, no matter how much I want for you to."

"I'd never heard of the Up-and-Under before we ended up here," said Avery. "I don't suppose it can be very easy to get here from our world."

"No, it's not easy at all," said Soleil. "There has to be a really good reason, or else the Forest doesn't go looking for people to bring over. The Queen of Wands can open the way if she wants to, and the Impossible City can do it without help if it *really* needs somebody to send on a quest. People who don't come from here don't know what's really impossible, and so they feed the City by doing things the wrong way. It's why the road will usually try to run them through all four of the Kingdoms. It's just bad luck for Zib that Fire came last, instead of something else."

"I guess," said Avery, thinking that if Earth had come last, he'd be the one being carried. Would Jack have volunteered to carry him the way he was carrying Zib? The bird-boy had always seemed to like Zib better, but Avery weighed more than she did, and he wasn't sure any of the others would have been able to lift him. The image of Zib and Niamh dragging him facedown through the muddy grass of Earth was enough to draw a single, involuntary bark of laughter from his lips.

Avery's ears reddened at the tips as his companions turned to look at him. Niamh looked concerned, Soleil curious, and Jack almost annoyed. Avery scuffed his toe against a blackened bit of ground, resisting the urge to duck his head in shame.

"Sorry," he said. "Just thought of . . . something funny."

"Keep your funny to yourself," advised the Page, swooping back to briefly fly beside him. "We're almost there."

As if her words had summoned them, the heat haze in the air ahead of the group cleared, resolving into a tall stand of close-set trees, their trunks pressed so tightly against each other that they very nearly formed a wall. They were crowned in glorious green, with no sign that they had ever known the burning of the world around them, and there was no possible way they could have survived in this place, or been this close a moment before.

Avery, who was learning more and more that the line between possible and impossible was only two letters long, bit his tongue and said nothing at all as the group continued onward toward the trees.

The Page got there first, of course. She circled the stand, leaving sparks in her wake that winked out as soon as they touched leaf or bark, and waited for the rest of them to catch up.

Jack was the second to reach the copse despite the burden of Zib hanging limply in his arms. He didn't hesitate, just ducked between the trees, sliding through a space that shouldn't have been wide enough to admit him, and was gone. Niamh was close behind, her shoulders relaxing as she stepped into the shade, clearly more comfortable out of the direct sun, however weak and watered-down that sun might be. Then came Soleil, with Avery only a few steps behind her.

Avery hesitated, watching the Page circle, as a certain terrible conviction gripped his heart and made it difficult to properly breathe. Whatever waited for them in that grove, whatever form it took, it was going to bring this piece of their journey to a close as surely as any other obstacle they had faced or overcome. He couldn't say he was truly happy here in the Kingdom of Fire, but it felt like their time in the Up-and-Under was coming to an end. Like a child who had been asking to go home from a relative's house since lunch, suddenly faced with the threat of actually going home, he realized he wasn't ready. There was so much they hadn't seen or done, so many mysteries unsolved and questions that would be left unanswered if things ended now. He hesitated, and the Page scowled as she watched him, waiting for him to follow the others into the trees.

Finally, with a tightness in his chest he couldn't quite articulate, Avery stepped between the trees and into the Candle Grove.

The trees formed a ring no more than three or four deep around a wide, grassy clearing dotted with yet more of those small white flowers and filled with lush shadows by the branches stretching overhead. The shadows didn't have time to settle into anything deeper, as the air above the grassy soil was filled with dancing sparks. They looked like the flames that Avery normally saw flickering atop candles, but with no candles to anchor them as they swirled and twisted through the air. Some were small enough to have topped birthday candles. Others were balls of flame large enough to have occupied torches.

Not all of them were floating, either. Some had settled on the branches overhanging the clearing, flickering warmly without burning or scorching the bark beneath them. Here, the flowers smelled of hot wax and burning oil, of firewood and burnt marshmallow. All the friendliest aspects of fire, and none of the more destructive.

The Page spun slowly in the air, spreading her arms to indicate the dance of flames around them. "They *did* come here!" she crowed, delighted. "Not all of them, maybe, but enough of them for burning! Oh, we can make a bonfire of this many citizens; we can warm ourselves proper, the way we're meant to do! We can burn again!" Then she sobered, the flames which had begun leaping from her hair dying back down to their normal simmering flicker. "But if the Queen's not here, all we'll do is burn for a moment and then blow out again. We need her to bring back

Fern, and we need Fern to burn without burning so much we burn away to nothing."

"Wait," said Avery, whose head was beginning to spin. "The owl is more important than a queen?"

"No, and yes, and no again," said the Page. "Everything's a hierarchy. Doesn't it work that way where you come from?"

"Not at all," said Avery.

"So if one important person disappears, there are no more important people left absolutely anywhere, and everything just falls apart?"

"No," said Avery, feeling even more lost than he had a moment before. "That would be ridiculous."

"The Queen lights the fires, and I serve the Queen," said the Page. "When she has to be away in the Impossible City, I stay here and make sure everything goes as it's meant to—it's why I'm so much more of a person than the other Pages. I have to be. If I'm element alone, I can't do all the things that need doing to keep a kingdom functional when its monarch isn't here, like feeding people and telling the sparks which rooms to clean—not that I've been doing that since they all blew out, but still, I *did,* until they went away. When she's done living in the Impossible City and keeping the light lit in the tower, she'll come back here and sit on her own proper throne, and I'll throw all my personhood away to be an element instead, and I'll burn, and I'll burn, and I'll burn!"

She laughed with delight at the very thought of that dreamt-of day, spinning in the air and wrapping her arms around her chest in a single-person embrace. The sparks from her hair lit up the grove even more than the darting flames had done, casting green stained-glass shadows through the bottoms of the leaves on the trees and painting the canopy with the skeletal outlines of branches.

Avery was so distracted watching her that he paid no attention to his companions, didn't notice as Jack carried Zib to an open stretch of ground and eased her gently down into the moss and flowers, didn't see as Soleil approached one of the trees, eyes huge in her half-familiar face, attention fixed on one dancing candle flame. Niamh, meanwhile, moved to the absolute center of the grove and held herself perfectly still, like she could convince the fire she wasn't there if she just didn't attract its attention.

The Page continued to spin, and Soleil continued to approach the fire on the tree, and everyone was moving, and no one was moving together.

Then two things happened at the exact same time.

Soleil reached out and brushed her fingertips against the flame in the tree, and gasped as it disappeared, winking out entirely. Another flame, drifting down from the canopy above, landed on Zib's chest and settled there, burning like a small, lambent ball of flickering white and blue. Zib sighed. It was the first truly audible sound she had made since her collapse, and every head turned toward her, even Soleil's.

"Zib?" asked Avery, moving toward his friend. His own eyes widened when he saw the flame at the center of her chest, and he turned back to the Page, frantic. "She's a human person, not an elemental person! It's going to burn her! You have to get it away!"

The Page drifted through the air toward Zib, confusion and concern in her expression. "That's not . . . I don't know that fire," she said. "That's not one of our citizens."

Zib sighed again, a little louder, the sound of a sleeper on the verge of waking up. Then she gasped and sat upright, the tiny bonfire still clinging to her chest like some strange sort of boutonniere. She looked around her, at the grove filled with dancing flames and shifting shadows, and her mouth worked soundlessly for several seconds, looking for all the world like she was chewing on her words. Finally, in a raspy voice, she said, "I went somewhere."

"You fell down, and when you hit the ground, you passed out," said Jack, moving back to her side. He crouched down, steadying her where she sat.

"Jack carried you all the way here," said Niamh.

"Where is here?" asked Zib.

"The Candle Grove," said Soleil. As her voice had changed when she went from being a Crow Girl, corvid collective emulating human form, to being a girl from side to side, it had changed again, growing smoother, older, richer with the layers that come only from time and memory. A person who is very young may sound thin and narrow to the ear, less because they lack the potential to one day be the deepest of thinkers, more because they do not yet carry the complexities of memory easy in their bones.

Zib looked at Soleil and gasped again, this time with wonder rather than with shock.

Avery and Jack both turned to look as well. Niamh did not. Niamh was born to the Up-and-Under, and she had recognized the shape of this story long since; she knew what she would see when she looked, and was at once gladdened and grieving at the knowing.

Her friend, such as she had been, was well and truly gone. Drowned girls do not have so many friends that they can lose one without grieving at least a little, even if those people will go on to live long and happy lives as whoever they've become. She had known from the moment of meeting them that she would lose Zib and Avery, who had only ever been visitors to the Up-and-Under, lost children of another world desperately seeking a path back to their parents; she still did not regard Jack as a friend, but as a potentially dangerous interloper to be watched with caution and offered only what kindness the situation demanded. The Crow Girl, though . . .

They had been very different from the beginning, one called to water and the other bound to air, one a victim of circumstance and the other of her own poor choices, but they had also been the same. Both of them had been human residents of the Up-and-Under, once upon a time. Both of them had been transformed by the world in which they lived, which was fickle and fond of changing things into new shapes, whether or not those things gave consent. They had been different and they had been the same.

That similarity had begun to fade when Soleil reclaimed her heart and, with it, her name, but she had still been missing so much of who she'd been that their differences had been outmeasured by their sameness. Now, though . . .

Niamh listened to Soleil speak, and closed her eyes, and did not turn to see what had happened to her friend.

What had always been inevitable.

TEN

WHAT THE FIRE
REVEALED

All those who *did* turn to see why Soleil sounded so odd froze, staring at the stranger in her place. There were still aspects of Soleil's bones in the new woman's face, as if this were one of many people the teen had been in a position to grow up to become. It was just unusual for someone to grow up in an instant, after touching a floating flame.

Her hair was no longer black seamed with red, but red, and orange, and white, and yellow, all blending together in a shimmering, ever-changing cascade of curls that fell down her back like a lava flow. Veins of black still ran through it, as if those were the spots where the burning color had come together and

solidified into stone. Unlike the Page, her hair didn't shed sparks; nor did it seem to end, but flowed downward to a point where the eye refused to look any closer and shied away.

The gown of black feathers she had worn when she was a Crow Girl and even after was gone, and in its place was a gown that matched her hair from the bottom to the hip, black at the base and burning through a hundred shades of red and yellow, only to move from white to purple, and several shades of blue as it approached her shoulders. She was not visibly burning. She looked like the birthing of a bonfire.

The Page gasped, adding her own surprise to the towering pile of surprises that had been waiting for them in the Candle Grove, and then, with no preamble, burst into tears. She shot across the distance between herself and Soleil like a stone from a sling, slamming into the much taller woman and wrapping her arms tight around her waist, sobbing into the side of her dress. Soleil smiled sadly and stroked the Page's burning hair, seeming untroubled by the sparks it shed.

"I'm sorry, darling," Soleil said. "I didn't mean to. I didn't understand what I was asking for, and more, I didn't see the trap as it was built around me—not until the jaws were snapping shut."

"What you were asking for?" The Page let her go in order to shy back in the air, confusion on her face wiping away her relief, although the tears remained. "You mean you *asked* to leave us?"

"I went to Anemone because I was tired of the weight of the pleas of the people on my heart. I feared it was making my choices worse than they deserved, because I was so conflicted. If one person begged for sunlight to strengthen their farm while another asked for rain to save their family, how was I to choose between them? How did I have the right? My own training had been scant to the point of scarceness. A crown, a coronation, and a throne to warm for how long? Forever? Whenever I asked, they'd just say, 'The Queen is in her parlor, the light is in the tower, and all is well with the world.' What if the Queen didn't *want* to be in her tower? What if a king were there instead? Would the Up-and-Under really come to ruin?"

"If it were the King of Cups or the Queen of Swords, yes, it would," said Jack. "I love my mother, as much as a heartless boy can love, but she would wreck the world to make herself just one more monster. And when she made a monster out of you, she gifted you to the King of Cups because she knew he wouldn't question where you'd come from. She is too arrogant and greedy, and he's too complacent and cruel. Only the King of Coins could do as fine a job as everyone says the Queen of Wands has done, and there's no profit in the crown: he will not have it."

"No profit?" asked Avery, who was feeling

distinctly as if he had missed something. Where was Soleil? Why were his companions speaking to her so . . . not deferentially, but as if they knew her?

The beginnings of an understanding were attempting to untangle themselves at the back of his mind, as if they knew that one day, people who had heard this story before would look at him and wonder how he could possibly have taken so long to understand. But Avery was a young boy from a place where people don't turn into other people at the dropping of a feather or the flickering of a flame, where hair doesn't dance with living fire, where kings and queens don't go walking among the common people of the world. He was also tired, and hungry, and thirsty, and had never in his life worn the same clothing for so long, from his threadbare shirt to his tattered trousers. He was doing his best in a very strange, unprecedented situation, and who among us can say that we would have snatched the answer from the air any more quickly than he did?

So as he frowned at Soleil, and Zib, still sitting on the grassy ground, blinked in absolute confusion, Soleil herself took a half-step toward him, her hands empty and open in front of her.

"I remember you properly now," she said. "All the way back to the beginning of knowing you, I remember you. Going from a queen to a crow stripped everything I had ever been out of me, and left me weak as a fledgling. Anemone didn't mention *that* would be the cost of what she offered." Her face darkened. "There will be a conversation about the law, and whether what she did was allowed beneath it. There may yet be a war."

"Not too terrible of one," said Jack, helping Zib to her feet. "Broom still spreads his wings across the Kingdom of Air, but Mother has no heir since she had my heart from me, and even if I were willing to trade my wings for the weight of a human heart, I was an infant when she stole it. I would know nothing, remember nothing of who I am. I grew up like this. I am entirely unsuited to rule."

"Then a little war," said Soleil in a placating tone. "Something to remind her that while she may be an excellent maker of monsters, she isn't the only one with teeth and talons."

The Page of Gentle Embers tugged on her sleeve, tugging her attention along with it. Soleil lifted her eyebrows as she turned to look at the younger girl.

"Yes?"

"My apologies for interrupting, but we came here to wake the child, and look." The Page gestured to Zib, who was leaning on Jack's arm, the tiny flame still burning at her breast. "The child is awake, and seems well enough for all that's happened to her thus far. The tower is dark. You *must* return to the Impossible City."

"And I can't go," said Niamh, finally turning around, with a look in her eyes like her heart was being broken.

"Of course you can go," said Soleil.

"Drowned girls are very possible," said Niamh. "I went the first time by the graveyard path, as I told you when the road was still with us. The path will not have me a second time."

"A drowned girl accessing the City a second time is entirely impossible," said Soleil. "It has never happened, not once in all the days of the Up-and-Under."

"Then I will stay here, in this dry and blasted place, until Fern returns from wherever the great owls go when they go missing, and then perhaps the Page and I can convince her to carry me back to the Salt-wise Sea and let me go."

"You aren't *listening*," said Soleil, for the first time sounding ever so slightly annoyed. "Anyone dead can take the graveyard path when they want to visit the City. But if they want to visit the City again, they have to find something even more impossible than a dead person following a road. The City will let you in because you're with me, and because it's impossible for you to come in a second time."

"Even more impossible than following a road," said Niamh, with slow wonder. "Was it always that easy?"

"Not if you were looking the rules head-on, but once you step to the side, yes."

Avery's temper caught like the fire burning at Zib's breast. He whirled on Niamh. "You said all the way back at the beginning that you couldn't go with us into the Impossible City, and so we walked away, and all this has happened because we followed you! You could have gone there any time you wanted to!"

"No, Avery, she couldn't have," said Soleil. "She had to move far enough into impossibility that the gates would open."

"And if you hadn't gone on this adventure, so many things wouldn't have happened," said Jack. "You found Soleil's heart! You found the Lady of Salt and Sorrow, and let her be one person again, when she'd been trapped as two for so long! You found the Page of Gentle Embers and made sure she wasn't alone anymore! You found me. I would still be a captive in my mother's cage if you hadn't come along to make me fly for freedom."

Zib put a hand on his arm, steadying him as he was steadying her, and looked to Avery, her own face pale and drawn, especially when compared to how brightly she normally burned. "We had to walk the improbable road long enough to make the impossible things possible," she said. "Sometimes it's about taking the journey on your own. It's why my daddy gets mad at me when I don't want to do my homework. He says it doesn't matter if I'm bored; I need to go through all the steps, or the ending won't make sense when I get there. We couldn't go straight to the ending when we were first setting out. It wouldn't have made any sense."

"Soleil's the Queen of Wands, and has been the whole time," Avery informed her.

"Yes," said Zib.

"Doesn't this *bother* you?"

"Why should it?" She shrugged. "Royalty in disguise happens all the time in the fairy tales, and this is sort of like a fairy tale, if you squint at it and take a few steps backward. She didn't lie to us, if that's why you're unhappy. She didn't know. Someone who says something that's true when they say it doesn't become a liar just because that thing changes."

Avery, who had not read many fairy tales, sagged and sighed, looking down at the toes of his scuffed shoes. "I want to go home," he said.

"This is how we do that," said Zib. She looked to Soleil. "Will the Kingdom of Fire be all right with you going back to the Impossible City, so you can let us in and send us home?"

"The embers have been banked, but they can be built back up again, now that we know where the Queen is," said the Page gleefully. "It'll be even faster if you can find Fern and send her home. We'll be blazing in no time!"

Zib, who still had a blossom of fire clinging to her

chest, nodded solemnly. "Then we're going to the Impossible City."

She didn't say "finally" or "at last." She didn't need to. All the air said them for her, as if the world were holding its breath. Soleil led the way to the edge of the grove, looking out across the blasted land-scape, which was already beginning to show signs of what passed for life here in the Kingdom of Fire—jets of flame were erupting upward every few feet, and pools of shimmering magma had begun to seep from cracks in the ground, gleaming like jewels in the smoke-filtered sunlight.

"Oh, well, this won't do at all," said Soleil with a small frown. She put two fingers in her mouth and whistled, as a woman might call an absent dog.

A ribbon of gleaming rainbow stretched across the hills and over the burning world, ending where the trees began. Soleil smiled as she stepped onto it.

"Thank you," she said, with deep sincerity. "You've done very well guiding the pieces of this puzzle to their places on the board, and now they're ready to slide home, all of them. We need to return to the Im-possible City. I've been absent too long. The light in the tower is out, and I'm told an army is being raised to take advantage of my absence."

"Wait," said Avery, voice sudden and sharp. Soleil looked at him, curious, and he looked back, defiant.

"If the King of Coins doesn't want to take the City because he can't profit from having it, why is he raising an army against it?"

"The King of Coins controls the earth, and stones make good soldiers," said Soleil, waiting for the rest of them to join her on the ribbon of the road. "He could be raising the army for either of the others, or for one of their Pages, if they were considering a challenge for the crown. A Page *can* challenge, when the circumstances are right. The City deserted, the tower dark—those might be the circumstances they'd need. Let them claim the City, pull its power into the element they embody, and then turn against the monarch they supposedly serve."

"I would *never*," said the Page of Gentle Embers, sounding scandalized.

"I know," said Soleil. "And you'll be staying here to reignite the Kingdom, anyway: you would never have volunteered to do that if you'd been plotting against me. You never would have let us into the palace if you'd been plotting against me. But the Page of Frozen Waters might plan insurrection, as a sort of game she can play against the entire world."

"Oh," said Avery.

They all began moving down the road, the Page drifting by Soleil's side as if reluctant to let the older woman out of her sight, leaving sparks dancing in the air. The improbable road twisted gently, bending around the jets of flame and the larval volcanos jutting from the earth, so that the group was able to walk without burning themselves. Niamh found a position at the center of the group, Soleil and Avery ahead, Jack and Zib behind, where she was shielded on all sides from the flaming landscape.

They had just crested the top of a small hill when Soleil stopped, turning to look at the Page with an expression of profound regret. "It's time," she said.

"But you just *got* here!"

"And you know why I have to go as quickly as I came. The tower is dark because I left it unattended. I was selfish and I was silly and I thought my own need for peace outweighed the needs of all the Up-and-Under. I have to fix what I've broken. That means *not* throwing the Kingdom of Fire even deeper into chaos in the process!"

The Page paused, a canny look coming into her eyes. "Perhaps the weight of the crown wouldn't press down so hard if you could find someone else to carry it for short times," she suggested, in a voice like a child wheedling for just one more cookie before bed. "It may be time to take . . . not a consort, but an advisor. Someone who will act only in your stead, and allow you to return home to refuel yourself."

"They would have to be aligned to fire, and unable to rule in their own right," said Soleil thoughtfully.

"If I find such a person, I will consider it. It would be pleasant to return home before my term is done."

"How long is a term?" asked Zib curiously.

Oddly enough, it was Niamh who answered, saying, "Each quarter claims the crown and holds it for as long as it suits the Up-and-Under. The last reign of Swords lasted the better part of a century, and ended only because the then–Queen of Coins took offense at the way the King's laws were impacting her profits. Air is hot and wet; earth is cold and dry. Either can defeat the other, but only if they take their opponent by surprise."

"Water can do the same to fire," said Jack. "When Soleil's reign ends, it will likely end because the King of Cups cares enough to challenge. Which is why this army is quite so concerning. If the Page of Frozen Waters seizes the City, she'll become a Queen in her own right, and the current King of Cups will fade away. Not only the Kingdom of Water but the whole of the Up-and-Under will belong to someone cruel and cold, and the world will change to suit her."

"We can't just pretend the army isn't there," said Avery. "But how long will we have to walk before we get to the City?"

"As long as the road requires," said Soleil. She blew the Page a kiss, and the girl snatched it out of the air and stuffed it into her mouth before turning a somersault and soaring away, back toward the palace, back into the blackened depths of the Kingdom of Fire.

Soleil smiled after her, looking entirely pleased and exceedingly fond, then resumed walking, leading the others down the other side of the rise. They were now crossing a less-seared plain, although the ground remained sunbaked and hard, with no signs of growth nor green. Smoke still stained the sky overhead, thinner here but no less present.

"How far are we from the border?" asked Niamh.

"Some distance," said Soleil. "Things have shifted in my absence. Nothing too unusual in *that,* but it makes it hard to say how long we might be walking."

"I'm tired," announced Avery. "We've been walking a long time."

"Have we?" asked Soleil curiously. When Avery nodded, she smiled. "I suppose you'd know better than I would. I'm still remembering what it is to walk any distance at all. I spent a great deal of time as a collection of crows. I'm more accustomed to flying."

"If the Page can fly, can't you?" asked Zib.

"No," said Soleil. "Pages are almost entirely element, hollowed out and left for the world to fill up as it will. The Pages of Fire and Air can always fly, as the Pages of Earth and Water can always dive deep into the element sustaining them and move through it as if it were nothing at all. I, however, am still far too occupied with being a person to be hollow enough to fly. I think . . ." Her expression turned wistful. "I think the thought of flying was what let me believe Serafina wouldn't wish me ill. We had never been friends, she and I—the monarchs of Swords rarely have friends—but we got on well enough, and I trusted her. Too much, as it turned out. She took more than I had offered. She took things that weren't hers to have, and she let the light in the tower go out."

"Oh," said Zib softly. She hadn't considered how much the Crow Girl had given up to become Soleil again—to become the Queen of Wands again. Freedom to be who she wanted to be and go where she liked. Freedom to *fly*.

Zib had never been able to fly, but she couldn't imagine having it and losing it and not mourning it for every day of her life.

The flower of fire still burned at her breast, bright and warm and not quite hot enough to scorch her when she plucked at it, distracted and anxious. She could feel that plucking all the way to her spine, like she tugged upon some essential piece of her own body, something so deeply rooted that it couldn't possibly be removed. She let her hand fall back to her side, not wanting to investigate that feeling any more deeply.

Avery was still walking, but slowly, not lifting his feet very far from the surface of the road. His shoulders were slumped, and he really did look utterly worn out, like this was the longest journey he had ever been asked to endure. Which, she supposed, if she took the whole of their time in the Up-and-Under as a single period, it was. She had never been on a trip this long before, either, and certainly not on foot! Why, they had walked most of the way around an entire world!

Jack stayed close by Zib as they walked, looking as if he expected her to fall down again at any moment. As Avery slowed more and more, Niamh drew level with Soleil, until their order had quite changed, water and fire in the front, air and fire in the middle, and earth bringing up the rear.

Soleil stopped. "This won't do at all," she said, turning to look at Avery with pursed lips and hands on hips. "Getting you children into the Impossible City only solves the situation if I can get you both there intact. Road, I will need you to stay just as you are, even as we step away. Land"—here she turned to address the bleak and seemingly near-lifeless countryside to her right—"I need you to see for us."

The effect was immediate and all but unbelievable. The soil churned as grasses and vines burst upward from it, the vines assembling themselves into the shapes of chairs and a round picnic table, the grasses creating a lush green carpet studded with more of those little white flowers. Bushes sprouted around the edges of the near-perfect circle this oasis of growth created, their branches groaning as they grew with unnatural speed, putting out leaves and tiny yellow blossoms that rapidly withered and dropped to the ground, replaced by equally fast-ripening fruit.

Berries in yellow, blue, red, pink, and even waxen white appeared, growing fat and inviting while they watched. As the growth slowed, Soleil stepped off the improbable road and moved toward the nearest pink-berried bush.

"Bonberries," she said, with some relish, and plucked a handful before settling in the first of the chairs. "Well? It's safe here, and you did seem to be saying that you needed a rest, Avery."

With a glad sound, her four companions joined her on the grass, Jack, Avery, and Zib filling their hands with fruit before they sat, Niamh falling facedown into the grass. It wasn't the boneless, motionless fall Zib had taken before; it was the gleeful flop of someone who had been out in the summer sun all day long finally offered the opportunity to slip into the shade. The grass, though new-grown, was cool and slightly damp, as if it had been wetted by the morning dew.

Zib stuffed berries into her mouth, heedless of the colors, exclaiming in delight at the new flavors. The pink bonberries were old, familiar friends by this point, but the others were entirely new, delights the Up-and-Under had not yet deigned to share with them.

Jack nibbled more delicately at his own berries, a mixture of white and blue, while Avery sat with full hands and wide eyes, trying to take everything in at once.

"How is this possible?" he asked. "This isn't fire."

"But it is," said Soleil. "Where the land burns, it grows back lush and green. The seeds of life are always hidden in the ashes of destruction. It takes a great deal for my kingdom to provide a respite such as this, and I would not ask for it were the need not great, but you are still a child from your America, and the world presses hard on you. You needed to be fed and feted, and given the opportunity to take your rest. My kingdom could provide such once, if not many times. When we leave, the fire will reclaim this patch. The berries left unpicked will give their seeds into the soil, and some of them will survive the burning. Next time the world needs to supply such a place, they will be ready for their moment in the sun."

"Oh," said Avery, and looked at the berries in his hands. "So these are safe for me to eat?"

"I may not be the girl I was when first we met and formed a friendship, but I remember being her, even if she never once remembered being me," said Soleil. "Yes, it's safe for you to eat anything I offer. Nothing will harm you if I have any say in it. Some things are beyond my control, and those may harm you, but the food here is safe as it can be."

"Does all the Up-and-Under answer to you like this?" asked Zib.

"Only my own lands and the City," said Soleil. "Everything else is outside my hands. I can't give Avery back the shine from his shoes, or give Jack back his heart. Those things were given into the custody of other forces."

"I don't want my heart back, anyway," said Jack. "I lost it before I knew what it was, and I saw what getting your heart back did to *you*." He waved a hand at Soleil, like he was trying to encompass everything she was with a simple gesture. "The Up-and-Under needs you, Your Majesty, but you're a queen as much as my mother is, and you can never be my friend. Not like the Crow Girl was. She was a singular person in the fullness of a flock, and I'll miss her as long as I'm capable of missing anyone."

"She was never real," said Soleil gently.

"Real and unreal are the same as possible and impossible; they're ideas, and what matters is where you're standing when you try to look at them," said Jack. "She was real when she was here with us, she was a person with her own ideas and experiences independent from the person she'd been when she was you, and we're allowed to miss her now that she's gone away."

Soleil sighed. "It is a mean thing, to condemn yourself to a life lived entirely without your heart."

"Why?" asked Jack. "I can fly, as long as I don't have a heart. I'll never be any older than I want to be, or any younger either, as long as I choose my birds with care. I'll never leave the people I care for without meaning to, and I'll never love anyone enough to do myself harm. I *can* still love. The heart is not the only place love lives. It lingers in all the humors, all the elements, and I have love as much as anyone does, but not the kind that eats you up alive."

"Love can do that?" asked Zib, who was young yet to understand that sort of love. All of us are that young once. It is not a state that lingers, but is very much a state to be enjoyed while it exists. Still, she looked at him with wide and earnest eyes, all innocent desire to understand.

Jack coughed into his hand. "Yes, it can, if you let it," he said.

"I won't," said Zib. "Not ever."

"Me, either," said Avery. He had eaten through most of his berries without really noticing, and was too tired to get up and pluck another handful. His eyes were beginning to droop, eyelids too heavy to hold open for another moment.

"So you say," said Soleil, not unkindly. "This is a safe place to stop and rest, and it may be the last such safety we see until we retake the City, so if you wish to sleep, you should close your eyes and sleep. I promise you, no harm will come to you in

135

my kingdom. The tower may be dark. The beacons of Fire are not."

That was all the invitation Zib needed. She slid out of her chair and down into the soft cool grass, curling on her side with one arm pillowed beneath her head, the flower of flame at her breast flickering softly as it reached upward. Avery put his head down on the table but remained in his chair, where he wouldn't be risking grass stains on his clothes. Niamh stood, walked a few feet away, and sat down cross-legged before falling over backward, once again pressing as much of herself as possible to the dewy ground. And Jack burst into birds, flying a slow circle overhead before he gathered on the branches and boughs.

Soleil watched them settle, her strange companions, and ate another berry, trying not to dwell on how she would soon betray them.

ELEVEN
THE CITY WALLS

Night never seemed to come to the Kingdom of Fire, not now that Soleil knew who she was; it was as if the sun itself, great burning beast of the sky, wanted to stay as close to her as it possibly could, enjoying her presence. So it was that while they slept for hours, the light was precisely the same when they woke. Soleil was sitting at the table in the same place she had been before, but had clearly moved during their slumber: a basket that seemed to be formed of black glass sat on the table, filled to the absolute brim with berries, so many that any jostle would send them spilling to the ground.

Zib was the first to open her eyes, sitting up and

rubbing the sleep away from them as she yawned enormously. She glanced down as she did, almost automatically, and stopped yawning—stopped breathing—as she saw the fire flower still flickering at her breast. She glanced up again, catching Soleil's eyes, and Soleil nodded, very slightly. Zib sighed as she looked down again, then planted her hands against the soil and pushed herself to her feet.

Zib's motion woke Avery, who lifted his head from the table and blinked blearily at the scene around him. Nothing had changed, and that seemed to surprise him somehow, as if he had been expecting, even after all this time, to be able to wake and wish the more fantastic elements of their adventure away, reducing them to something out of a dream. His face fell, marking his disappointment, and he put his head back down, tensed shoulders revealing that he hadn't gone back to sleep.

Niamh sighed and stood, going from sleep to wakefulness without any stops between, and as she did, Soleil looked at her and said, "You have slept two nights in the Kingdom of Fire, child of Water, and that is another impossible thing to buy you entrance to the City."

"If I get enough, maybe I can pay the crossing cost," said Niamh.

The sound of voices woke the jackdaws clustered in the bushes, and they rose in a flurry of wings and croaking caws, swirling back together in the shape of a boy at the center of the grassy patch. Jack looked exactly as he always had, entirely himself as he moved to stand behind Zib, watching Soleil with sharply alert eyes, as if he expected her to change again at any moment.

Instead, she rose, picking up her basket of berries, and moved back toward the shimmering line of the improbable road.

"We should keep going, now that you're all rested and we have some provisions for the journey," she said. "It won't be that much farther now, and my kingdom can't sustain this place forever."

"Did you sleep at all?" asked Niamh.

"A king or queen in their own territory has no need for sleep," said Soleil. "The light is not currently in the tower, but the light still shines."

"Ah," said Niamh, and moved reluctantly toward the edge of the grassy space, Zib and Jack behind her. Only Avery remained where he was, facedown on the table.

Soleil set a gentle hand on his shoulder. "It's time," she said.

"It's not," he said.

"One of us is right and one of us is wrong, and soon enough we'll know the difference," she said. "When the grass is gone and the chair beneath you turns to ashes, who will be correct, do you suppose?"

Avery finally lifted his head to glower at her. "I'm still tired. We haven't stopped for long enough."

"I know endings are frightening things, but this one has been delayed long enough. Come." She took her hand away, following the others to the road.

At last, Avery rose and moved to join the group. He glanced back as he did, and saw that the grass at the edges of the circle had begun to blacken and char, withering as if the whole of autumn had arrived at once. The branches of the berry bushes drooped, dropping their leaves to the ground as the heat came for them as well. He turned back to Soleil.

"I am sorry," she said. "This was inevitable. I held it open for as long as I could, to let you all rest, but the fire will always return. Of all the elements, fire is the one that dies to live again, and here, it rules all it touches."

"I know," said Avery, voice gone dull. "I'm just tired."

"This will all be over soon." Soleil placed her hand on his shoulder, and the group began following the road toward the line of the horizon, letting it serve as a destination until something more appeared.

And then, bit by shining bit, something more did appear.

The land around them did not change all at once like the edge of a knife, or like the shore between the Saltwise Sea and the Kingdom of Air. Even going from the Kingdom of Earth to the shore had been abrupt, assisted as it had been by the help-kelp sleeping in the well. For the first time in the Up-and-Under, things around them changed by degrees, the smoke beginning to clear overhead, the ground showing signs of life beyond the tiny white flowers they had seen before.

The road was tending gradually upward, and because every other change had been so slow and gradual, it was a shock to almost all of them when they finally topped the rise and beheld the Impossible City in all its distant, glimmering glory. As before, it was a confection of towers and spires and twisting, delicate peaks, impossibly tall, impossibly dainty, their heights connected by narrow bridges like loops of cobweb, strung with balls of light like drops of morning dew. From their new perspective, no longer newcomers to the Up-and-Under, Avery and Zib could see that one tower stood taller than any of the others, the central spire around which the rest of the City extended. In that tower, unlike the others around it, there were no lights: the windows stared dark and empty out upon the verdant landscape around the city.

The first time they had come close enough to see the Impossible City, it had seemed to rise out of the landscape without disturbing so much as a single blade of grass, urban area sprouting upward like a mushroom or a tree, entirely natural, part of a seamless whole. Now, looking with the eyes of experience, they could see that the land around it was divided into four distinct quarters, and each of them was slightly different from the others. The Impossible City still looked completely natural, but now it seemed less like the kind of nature they understood, and more like the city had somehow managed to transform the land around it to suit its own nature, immutable and absolute as it was.

It was still beautiful. Nothing about that had changed.

Soleil sighed, a deep and relieved sound that came up all the way from the bottom of her bones. "I was worried that somehow, it might be gone," she confessed. "I thought it might have disappeared."

"If the Impossible City were gone, the entire Up-and-Under would go with it," said Niamh. "Are you *sure* it's going to let me in?"

"Everything about this moment is impossible," said Soleil. "The gates will open for you, and you will be allowed within. We all will."

She started walking again, and the others followed, letting the road guide them down the slope of the hill, finally out of the Kingdom of Fire. The ground around them remained spangled with tiny white flowers. Zib could see drops of dew shining on the individual blades of grass, bright as diamonds in the sun. Still they walked on, and as they did, the sound of people drifted to them on the wind. Whoever they were, they sounded angry, voices raised in argument, underscored by the sound of metal clashing against metal.

Avery and Zib exchanged a glance. Soleil sighed again, less out of relief this time, more out of weariness.

"We were told of the army," she said, continuing to walk. "The sound of combat is not necessarily a sign of fighting, when an army is involved. They must train, to be ready when the fight does arrive, and this is a show of arms more than anything else. The Impossible City employs no standing army of its own. It's impossible that a hostile force should pass our walls, and so this army can surround us, can stop the passage of food and people, but cannot enter until and unless the City declares its general the victor."

"So it's a war of . . . waiting?" asked Zib.

"In a sense," said Soleil.

"But I thought all impossible things were possible here, so shouldn't the army be able to get in?" asked Zib.

Soleil paused, seeming briefly taken aback. Then she shook her head, calming. "No truly impossible city is possible, which makes it impossible, which makes our walls impassable," she said. "The possibilities cancel one another out, and they cannot enter."

Zib, who still wasn't sure she understood, frowned, but didn't argue any further. They continued on, and the army appeared before them.

At first glance it seemed like two different and distinct armies, fighting against each other. Upon looking closer, however, it was obvious to the eye that there *were* two armies, one clad in sparkling cloth dyed a dozen gemstone hues, the other dressed in white and blue, but they were not fighting one another. The swords that clashed were raised in pursuit of training. Figures prowled between the two companies, hands folded behind their backs and swords at their own hips, barking words of encouragement or critique. A line of tents sketched the shape of the training grounds, and as Avery watched, one of the soldiers took a blow to the arm and was waved off the field. He trotted toward the tents. The others moved to fill the gap created by his absence. The mock battle went on.

"There are so many of them," said Zib, sounding awed and a little bit frightened.

"There would have to be, if the Up-and-Under is going to war," said Soleil wearily. She kept walking, following the gleaming ribbon of the improbable road, which cut straight across the training ground, weaving and bending to avoid the clusters of people. None of them seemed to have noticed the group, and even as they moved back and forth, swords swinging and clashing against shields, none of them stepped onto the surface of the road. It was like it, and everyone who walked upon it, was protected somehow from prying eyes.

Niamh slowed when they were halfway across the field, eyes going wide, first with shock, then with recognition, and finally relaxing into resignation. It was a complicated expression, and only Jack saw it happen. He frowned, looking at her closely.

"Are you all right?" he asked.

It was the first time any of them had spoken since Soleil led them onto the training ground, and Zib and Avery both tensed, waiting for the soldiers to finally take notice of their presence. It didn't happen, and they began to relax as they continued following Soleil toward the city walls.

Jack, meanwhile, was watching Niamh, who was walking slower and slower, that expression of resignation not leaving her face. "What's wrong?" he asked, and that must have been the better question, because she finally turned to face him, bleak despair in her eyes.

"We were," she said. "It isn't the Page at all. This is *his* army, *his* assault, and we've led her right to him."

Jack recoiled, almost stumbling off the edge of the road before Niamh's hand shot out and grabbed him by the wrist, jerking him toward her.

"Do not leave the road," she hissed through gritted teeth. "The improbable road only protects the people who walk it. Go to birds and he'll see you in a second. Step onto the grass and he'll see you faster than that."

"He *who*?" asked Avery, who couldn't help but overhear when he stood so close.

"The King of Cups," said Niamh, releasing Jack as she turned toward Avery. "This is *his* army, *his* assault, and he may well have the power to take the City. We have to leave. We have to leave *right now*. Your Highness"—it was the first time she had addressed Soleil so, and for all that it was accurate, hearing it made Avery's chest feel tight, like something had just irreparably changed—"we have to go. We can take refuge . . . somewhere. The Forest of Boundaries, maybe. It protects those with nowhere else to go."

But Soleil was no longer listening. She was no longer walking, either. She had stopped dead on the road, one hand clasped over her mouth and the other clutching her stomach, as if she were about to be physically ill. Zib stepped forward, trying to see what Soleil saw.

The road bent again ahead of them, forming a sharp curve as it turned toward the city walls. On the green beyond the road's edge was another tent, larger than the rest, blue-sided, with white pennants flying above it. Not the white of surrender, no: they might have seemed that shade from a distance, but looking any closer showed that they were shot through with silver and with the very palest possible shade of blue. An army could march under those flags and never be breaking the laws of engagement, even as they skirted right against the edges of a lie.

A woman was standing outside the tent, picking her nails with the tip of a jagged dagger that appeared to have been made entirely from frozen water. Not ice—ice would have had a different texture to it, a solidity that would last until it melted. No, this was a slice of water, somehow frozen without freezing, turned into a weapon. It made sense, given the person who was holding it.

She was tall and slim and had the impeccable posture of someone who had been hit with a ruler every time she stooped or slouched since she was a very small child. Her hair was a deep gray, the color of charcoal but not quite true black, and her eyes were the color of fog, and her skin was a few shades lighter than that, a gray that could belong to nothing human, not even to waterlogged and long-drowned Niamh, who walked through the world dripping and pale. She was beautiful the way a hunting hawk is beautiful: as an afterthought, a warning. The sight of her was enough to stop both Avery and Zib in their tracks, both of them staring at the Page of Frozen Waters and not moving a single muscle they could consciously control.

She was not, however, the target of Soleil's gaze.

Between the road's edge and the woman outside

the tent stood a massive cage. It had bars of black iron, rimed with ice, that must have been so cold they burned. And in the cage huddled a massive owl. It would have been the largest owl any of them had ever seen, had they not already seen Oak, and Broom, and Meadowsweet. This owl, with its feathers as black as the iron bars around it, was clearly of their kind.

Steam rose from its body as it huddled there, like it was a cinder only recently extinguished. Avery glanced at Soleil, the first motion he had made since seeing the Page, and saw that tears were gathering in her eyes, pooling bright as diamonds at their edges. As he watched, they broke free and began to run down her cheeks, only to sizzle away into nothing before they could reach her chin. They left salty stains behind them.

He could almost see the moment when Soleil convinced herself to move. "Fern!" she shouted. The Page's eyes snapped from their casual study of the land around her to the black-haired woman who was now racing across the grass, her feet leaving smoking footprints behind her.

The great black owl stirred, opening shockingly purple eyes and fixing them on Soleil. It clacked its beak and ruffled its wings, all without moving from the very center of its perch, well away from the bars.

The Page spun her frozen-water dagger between her fingers like a small baton, moving toward Soleil with a smooth, easy stride. She looked unhurried and unconcerned, a small smile tugging at the corners of her mouth.

Soleil, meanwhile, was heading straight for the cage, slowing when she was close enough to reach out and touch the bars, pulling her hands back like the thought of touching them was absolutely unendurable. "Fern," she moaned. "What have they *done* to you?"

"Only caught and caged and kept me," said the owl in a voice that creaked like an unoiled gate, rusty with disuse and rough with damage. It was sweet for all of that, feminine and soft around the edges, as welcoming as the flicker of a flame. "The light went out in the tower."

"The Queen is in her parlor, the light is in the tower," said the Page, sing-song and sharp as a blade. "The clock is in the attic, chiming out the hour. And all the children wild and free and all the ladies pretty are putting on their dancing shoes and heading for the City." Then she bowed, deep as anything. "Hello, Your Majesty. You haven't been terribly missed."

Soleil looked to the Page, her own eyes narrowing in fury. "What have you done?" she demanded. "You have no right to imprison the Owl of an element not your own! Release her at once!"

"You wish to speak to me of rights, little cinder-girl who ran from flame to flue because she was so afraid of becoming a flicker when she used to be a blaze? You wish to tell me what I am and am not allowed to do?" The Page bared her teeth. "I have never once been yours to command. There's no fire in my heart. Even if there were, I swore my fealty to a sharper sword—and the King of Cups always wins, when he decides he's ready to play. He's playing now. You stepped away from your duties, and now he's ready to snuff you out like the candle you always were."

Her almost-snarl shifted smoothly into a smile, poisonously sweet and nowhere near her eyes. "But he's a merciful King. He'll spare your life, if you kneel before him and drink from his chalice."

"If I drink from his chalice, I'll blow out like I was never anything at all, and even my name will be forgotten."

"You gave it away for a pair of wings, once. Why is this so different?"

Soleil scowled. "You know it's not the same. You were cruel to me when I wore feathers. Did you know who I was?"

The Page flipped her frozen-water blade over in her hand, still smiling. "You can change your face and change your character, but your reflection always knows."

"Release my Owl."

"No."

"Then this is a declaration of war."

Avery flinched as the Page burst into laughter, high and bright and mocking, the sound dancing over the tentpoles and dueling soldiers. When she stopped laughing, every soul in the fields had turned to face her, their faces filled with dread and anticipation. Zib shifted closer to Jack, shivering. The day wasn't cold, and neither was she, but she shivered all the same.

There is a certain coldness to those whose hearts are frozen, and the Page held that coldness in her laughter, for her heart was frozen in both the emotional and the literal senses. Like Niamh, she had begun her strange existence as a living human girl, and like Niamh, she had fallen into deep, unforgiving water, sinking deep and deeper until there was no air left in her lungs, no fire left in her heart. Unlike Niamh, no one had come to find her, lost creature that she was, leaving her bones to roll like dice along the bottom of the sea until the King of Swords had come along and gathered her up, remaking her in his own image. That was where her similarity to Niamh, or to the Lady of Salt and Solace, ended. The Page was not a drowned girl for one simple reason:

Unlike the drowned girls, she no longer knew what it was to love. She had no room left inside her watery bones for anything but the cold anger she carried with her always, the anger she directed at a world that had allowed her child-self to drown. That anger carried on her laughter like smoke on a breeze, and all around her breathed it in, and felt themselves sickened by it, although they could not have said exactly why.

When she stopped laughing, it was as if a dark cloud had been covering the sun and had now passed on, leaving light to come back into the world. There was no time for any of them to sigh in relief, however, for she was moving closer to Soleil, blade bright in her hand. "What part of the army at your gates didn't you see as a declaration of war already, *Your Majesty*? What part of our presence escaped you? We have an army. You have four children. We have the Great Owl of your element. You have the fire banked in your breast, and not enough of that. You have nothing."

"We have the improbable road," said Soleil.

The Page cocked her head, looking for a moment honestly curious. "Do you?" she asked.

Soleil froze, stiffening where she stood like she had become as frozen as the blade in the Page's hand. Then, slowly, she turned back to face the others.

Then she screamed.

The screams of a queen are terrible things. Oh, queens can rage and queens can mourn, just the same as anyone else; the heart of a queen can shatter. This, however, was a scream of fury and disbelief, and it caused her companions to look down at their own feet, only to find that they were no longer standing on the iridescent ribbon of the improbable road. Instead, they stood on ordinary grass and ordinary mud, abandoned by their one constant guide.

The Page smiled again, terrible thing that she was, and drew back as if to strike, serpent in a terrible garden. A voice from behind stopped her.

It was male, terribly weary, as if the speaker had only just awoken from a longed-for nap, and wanted nothing more than to go back to their sleeping. "What are you doing, Page?" he asked. "I didn't request a regicide today."

"Majesty." The Page of Frozen Waters turned, her blade vanishing into her clothing as if it had never been there to begin with, and dropped into a deep and solemn curtsy. "My apologies. You said we were to go to war, and I thought—"

"There are two problems with what you've just said," said the man who had appeared at the mouth of the large tent on the other side of the field, which was terribly far away and suddenly felt impossibly close, like distance had managed to bend inward on itself while no one was looking. "First, that you thought. Your purpose isn't thinking, child. Your purpose is killing. Death by silver or death by water, it's all the same to me. If this were a kinder time, I would trade you for another Page—I've done it before, you know. You're nothing more than the foam atop a wave, and I can make another of you whenever I like."

"I know, I know," said the Page, sounding almost meek for once, like she had finally remembered that she wasn't just something that frightened, she was something that could be afraid.

"I don't think you do, actually," said the King of Cups—for of course it was he. It could have been no one else in all the world. He looked as old as ever, ancient and weathered until there was little left of him but skin clinging to bones like a canvas sheet wrapped around the bones of a sunken ship. Sheets of ice covered his skin and hair, cracking and falling loose when he moved, and where he walked, the grass browned and withered away.

Avery thought something was wrong with that. The King of Cups represented water—he understood enough about the elemental divisions that controlled this world to understand that. But water nurtured plants. Water was more than freezing and drowning. Water was warm rains and floating in the river; water was good crops and hot baths. Something in the King was missing. Maybe it was his Lady—but no, they'd brought her home to him. They'd reunited the whole Court of Cups, and things hadn't gotten any better.

"The second thing you got wrong is this," continued the King. "*I* never said that we were going to war. *I* never said that I wanted to go to war. The wheel turns, child. The thaw approaches."

Niamh gasped at that, clapping her hands over her mouth, and for a moment, the King glanced at her; for a moment, he saw her, and that terrible frozen face seemed to thaw, just a little, softening into something that might once have remembered how to be kind. Then he looked back to the Page, and his face hardened again, all the more terrible because it had shown that it could be something softer.

"The Impossible City is a dream," he said. "It belongs to someone who has no interest in material things, no desire to live in the world—no care for their own quarter. I have all those things. I have a Queen again, and I desire to stay with her. I don't want to take the City. You do."

"I do," said the Page. "I truly, truly do. You foolish old man. Why couldn't you have forgotten that you weren't the one to call for war? Why couldn't you have let the wheel be frozen?"

The King of Cups frowned at her, and was still frowning when the Page moved.

She moved like the water she was made from, elegant and swift, the blade back in her hand before she had even finished straightening, the same blade buried in the chest of the King of Cups before it seemed possible. He looked down at it, ancient eyes widening slightly with surprise, and then he fell, collapsing to the grass as if boneless. He didn't move again. Zib screamed, high and shrill, and the Queen of Wands was screaming too, and the Page was once more in motion, and the Queen of Wands was falling, falling, and they weren't on the improbable road any longer, and they were never going to make it to the Impossible City, and they were never going to go home.

And then the Page was smiling, and none of that mattered. Not really.

TWELVE
THE GRAVEYARD PATH

"I win," said the Page of Frozen Waters, smug and self-satisfied as she flipped her unbloodied knife over in her hand. "You lose."

Then she turned and walked away from them, leaving the children to stare at the two fallen monarchs.

Niamh was the first to move. She rushed to the side of the King of Cups, dropping to her knees as she folded her ever-damp hands over the wound in his chest. "Please, Majesty," she sighed. "Please. You said the thaw was coming. Thaw for me. Please."

"Niamh, he's gone," said Avery, starting toward

her. "Death doesn't work like that when it's people. You can't just beg him back to life."

Zib, meanwhile, was walking toward Soleil like she was asleep and didn't know what to do beyond walking. She reached up as she walked, closing her hand around the flame that had been burning at her breast since she woke in the Kingdom of Fire.

When she reached Soleil, she knelt, only to stop as a hand grasped her shoulder. Looking back, she saw Jack standing there, watching her closely, agony in his eyes.

"Do you understand what you're doing?" he asked.

"No," said Zib with open honesty. "But it's what the fire wants from me, and I don't know what else to do, and Soleil can't be dead, she just can't be dead. It's not allowed. If she's dead, we never make it into the City, and if we don't make it into the City, Avery never gets to go home."

Jack, who had noticed that she didn't include herself in that accounting, took a small step back and said nothing at all, only watched with aching sorrow as she pulled the flower from her chest and placed it on Soleil's.

Two things happened then, and they happened both at the same time, at the same instant, so that there was no difference between them at all. Even

Jack, who was watching closer than anyone, couldn't have said whether one happened before the other.

Zib released the blossom of fire, leaving it to flicker above Soleil's chest, clinging there as it had clung to Zib. Then her eyes rolled back in her head, and she fell limply to the ground as Soleil opened her own eyes and began to sit up.

Seeing Zib on the ground, she made a small sound of confused distress. Avery's shout was much louder. He rushed forward, toward the trio, dropping to his knees.

"Zib? Zib, wake up!" He grabbed her shoulders, shaking her briskly back and forth. Her head lolled, and her eyes remained closed. Her chest neither rose nor fell.

"I'm sorry," said Soleil, clasping her hands over her mouth. "I'm sorry, I didn't expect her to— I didn't think she could— I'm sorry."

"What did you *do*?" demanded Avery. "Why won't she wake up? What did you do to her?"

"She died in the Kingdom of Fire," said Jack, his own voice dead as dust. "The fire knew her for what she was, and took her for its own, all the way back there. When we went to the grove to reclaim Soleil's memory, Zib's own fire came back to her, but it didn't anchor all the way in body and bone the way it would have been before it was first shaken loose.

It could have, given time. There wasn't time. There's never enough time."

"She gave her fire to me," said Soleil. "She can't have known . . . Oh, Avery. Oh, Zib. I'm so sorry."

There was guilt in her voice, under the grief, for she had known, of course, that there would be a fight of some kind at the City gates; there always was, when you left and tried to come home. She had known that someone would fall, and had been intending to push one of them before the blade, for they were not a part of the functioning of her kingdom, of her land.

But there is a difference between a slaughter and a sacrifice, and she had never been given her proper opportunity to betray. So she, who might have been a villain, must remain a hero, and carry all the weight that that entails.

"Don't be," said Jack. "It's no punishment, to be a drowned girl."

At the same time, only a few feet away, Niamh was pressing her hands down upon the King of Cups like she thought she could heal his wounds with pressure alone. She bowed her head, hair hanging to hide her face, and whispered a final "Please."

Like the Queen of Wands before him, the King of Cups opened his eyes.

He sat up with a vast cracking sound, like ice shattering on a distant pond, and as the King moved, the ice coating his clothing and skin broke and fell away, leaving him young again, glowing with health, with no signs of the wound which the Page had opened in his chest. Niamh pulled back, eyes wide and amazed, her hands flexing helplessly as he pulled away from her.

Without saying a word, he rose from the ground and walked to the small cluster of people around the motionless Zib. He stopped next to Soleil, who looked up at him, tears steaming on her cheeks.

"Ah," he said. "A drowned girl, then?"

"A burning girl," she said. "I didn't think she would— I didn't expect her to— I didn't mean for any of this to happen!"

"We never do," he said, and reached down to offer her his hand. When she took it, he pulled her to her feet, letting her lean against him. "But the Up-and-Under always takes its due. Do you have any of Earth among your company?"

"Me," said Avery. "Or they said, anyway, that I'm full of earth. I still don't see how anyone can be full of just one thing, and not anything else at all."

"Not Earth enough, then," said the King. "A pity the King of Coins didn't come to join the fracas. We might have been able to recruit him to our aid."

"I have something better than Earth," said Jack, and reached into his chest like a man reaches into a cupboard, his arm sinking through flesh and bone to vanish into the very substance of his self. When he pulled it out again, he was holding a bird in his hand.

Not a jackdaw or a crow, either of which might have been expected, but a black-and-white bird whose feathers gleamed oddly blue in the light. It cocked its head, looking around itself with bright, keen eyes.

"I stole this from my mother's cages before we fled her kingdom," he said. "She's never been a part of anyone before, but she would be glad to have a flock. She told me so, while she slept in the aviary of my heart. If Zib hasn't traveled too far down the graveyard path by now, we might be able to call her back."

"Just get her back," commanded Avery.

Fern hooted in distress, still prisoned in the cage where the Page of Frozen Waters had sealed her. The King of Cups moved toward her, reaching for the bars with his newly youthened hands. Fern shied away, hooting again, even as Jack bent toward Zib, the bird still firmly in his hand.

"Getting her back won't free her, you know," he said, with one last glance at Avery. "She's a burning girl now, and she'll be a Magpie if this works, and either way, she'll be a creature of the Up-and-Under always and ever more. When you go home from here, you'll go on alone, and all of this will be a strange story you'll tell to your children someday, in the far-off country where you have them for your own."

"No," protested Avery. "I can't go back without her. I can't— She lives on my street! If I go back without her, they'll know something bad happened!"

"Were you friends, then, before the wall?" asked Jack, as he leaned closer still to Zib's unmoving shape, as he slipped the bird in his hand into her breast, letting it roost and settle there. "Did you play in the fields together, build snowmen, while away your hours?"

"We met at the wall," said Avery dully.

"Then the Up-and-Under brought you together, because it needed one of you to learn a lesson, and one of you to *be* a lesson. It seems the roles are set." Jack stepped back, away from Zib, straightening as he went. "I would have done it the other way around, if anyone had asked me. Let *her* carry the truth of what we are and what we serve back to your America. Let you walk the graveyard path and stay forever down among the dead and the drowned."

Zib took a great, shuddering breath and rolled onto her side, hacking and coughing like her lungs were preparing to burst. Avery cried out, a low, wordless sound, and moved to steady her. She turned her face away from him, and when this tilted her eyes toward Soleil, she screwed them shut, denying the sight of any of them.

"No," she said. "I didn't mean it. No, no, no." And between each word she spat out either a cinder or a feather, a burning thing or a tiny slice of sky.

"Drowning is hard," said Niamh, walking over and reaching down to guide her off the ground. "Drowning without water is harder."

Zib let herself be lifted. "No," she said again.

"You made the choice, Hepzibah. You could have chosen to let the light in the tower blow out in exchange for your own candled heart, but you chose the Queen. You chose the regent who will see us all protected over the one who would see us washed away."

The remade King of Cups looked briefly ashamed at that, and said nothing, only produced a key from inside his shirt and bent over the lock of Fern's cage.

"Choices have consequences, and they can't always be taken back."

"I didn't know," said Zib.

"But you did. Even if not all of you knew, part of you did, because part of you told the rest of you what to do. You listened when it spoke. You chose, Zib, and now you get to see what happens next."

"What do you . . ."

"Look for the path. It's waiting for you."

Zib frowned at Niamh, then turned around, squinting at the grass around them. The door to Fern's cage was swinging open, and the great blue owl was stepping out, shaking the fear from her feathers like dust, or ashes.

And Zib saw the path.

If the improbable road was a rainbow ribbon, this was its dark twin, a twining twist of black-and-gray iridescence stretched across the landscape. Upon seeing it, she could think of nothing she wanted more in all the world than to walk it, to see where it would take her if she followed it to its dim and distant end. She took a step forward, and then another, and then another after that, and the others watched her go, Jack moving to hold Avery back so he couldn't grab her arm, couldn't stop her.

The graveyard path beckoned, and Zib, finally able to see it for what it was, to understand its sweet allure, went willingly. It gleamed in the fading sunlight, and she stepped up onto it, onto the dark beauty of the road that called the dead, and she faded from the view of the living, disappearing into the space where only the dead can go.

Niamh, who was still a drowned girl, even if the graveyard path was no longer open for her, watched in silence, and if some of the moisture running down her ever-damp cheeks was from tears and not the memory of the sunken city where her heart belonged, who would ever know? Who would ever tell?

Zib walked away, into darkness.

THIRTEEN
THE IMPOSSIBLE CITY

The graveyard path is ever open to the dead who wish to undertake their first and most important journey. Some will use it to return home, to families and loved ones. Others will use it to pursue their ideas of a reward. Zib could have walked all the way back to America, had it occurred to her to do so.

But no one had told her any of those things. She had been told only that the graveyard path allowed the dead access to the Impossible City, and so she walked with quick, sure steps, until between one footfall and the next, the road beneath her was no longer gleaming with black fire, but was instead a

street of ordinary cobblestone. She stopped, eyes wide, and turned to look around.

The Impossible City is impossible in many regards, and one of those is the impossibility of properly describing it. Those who have been there can agree on two basic facts: first, that it is a city. It could be nothing else, with its shops and its streets and its citizens and its homes. It is a city of many souls, of many stories, each of them telling themselves over and over again, perfecting their designs. Secondly, that it is perfect. This is where the complication enters. Perfection for Avery would be straight lines and orderly districts, everything in its place and clearly intended to be exactly so. Zib's perfection was a wilder thing. When she beheld the City, it was color and motion and sound, the people laughing and dancing as they went about their business, the parks which dotted the thoroughfares growing wild with a thousand kinds of flower. Twinkling holiday lights were wound through the trees and along the eaves of buildings, and while she couldn't have named a single thing she saw displayed in the shop windows, every single one of them was a wonder and a delight, and something she could have spent her whole life in gazing upon.

She stood within the Impossible City, as impossible as the world around her, and the Impossible City moved over and through her, and she was, for a moment, content.

It is important to note that Zib was as yet quite young, no longer an infant or a toddling babe, not yet near the halcyon heights of her teenage years. To her, the idea of her own death was an impossibility, as impossible as the City around her. More so, even, for she could no more envision a world in which she was not, than a fish can envision an ocean with no water, or a bird envision a sky with no air. To children as yet too young to understand their own mortality, death was a subject for storybooks, a threat to be issued against the very ill or the very old.

There have always been children to whom this description does not apply, children unlucky enough to be born to ailing parents, or to ail themselves, while yet too young to carry their comprehension openly. Now that she found herself among the number of those gone to an early grave, Zib looked at what had happened to her, looked at the place inside her chest where once a flame had flickered and now a magpie began its nesting, shrugged, and let her feet lead her onward.

Much as the improbable road had bent and twisted to lead three children, a boy of birds, and a missing Queen across the Up-and-Under, the graveyard path pulled Zib along as it began to move, rolling across the more ordinary streets and cobblestones—if anything within the City could be considered "ordinary"—to deposit Zib by the City gates.

There were two men standing at attention there, both wearing curious uniforms that were four entirely different colors, one for each arm and each leg, and large, wooly hats that reminded her of caterpillars getting ready to hibernate in the fall. They held long staves with axe-shaped blades at one end, their eyes fixed rigidly ahead at the distance.

"Er, hello," said Zib.

"Oh, they can't answer you," said one of the men, his lips not moving. Zib blinked, and blinked again as that man's hat lifted its head and looked at her, great black eyes glinting like jewels in the light. "They're just doorkeepers. They keep the doors, and they keep anyone from opening them without consent of the Queen. But she's not given consent to anyone in days and days spilling over into months and months, and so they can't answer you."

"But she *did* give me consent," said Zib, and stomped one bare foot against the paving. It made the smallest slapping sound, barely loud enough to matter. "She's right outside the gates, and she told me to come and get the doors open so she could come back inside."

The second guard's hat lifted its head, twisting around so that it was looking at her entirely upside-down. "That's not possible," it said in a prim, higher-pitched tone. "The Queen is in her parlor, the light is in the tower, and all is—"

"Right with the world, except that it *isn't*," interrupted Zib. "It isn't right at all, because the Queen of Wands gave up her heart to the Queen of Swords so she could forget her burdens for a little while, and she forgot too much. She became someone else entirely, and it took a long time and a lot of trouble and some light theft for us to turn her back into who she *was*. So now she's your Queen, and she's outside your stupid City, because the Page of Frozen Waters scared away the road we were on, and I was the only one who could take the graveyard path, so they sent me in here all by myself! And now Avery can't go home unless you *listen to your Queen* and open up the doors!"

Zib was panting by the time she finished, all her air expended on the effort of trying to make them understand. Her chest ached, which seemed a little unfair to her: she was dead, wasn't she, to be able to walk the graveyard path? She had died in the Kingdom of Fire, and continued onward for a while after that, too startled by her own nonexistence to lie down and let the universe have her, until she had given her last hope of resurrection away to a Queen. Now she was a burning girl, and there was a magpie roosting in her rib cage where her heart was meant to be, and she was never going home.

That last was only now beginning to sink in. She could get this door open, could grant her companions access to the Impossible City—but would that access extend to her? According to Niamh, a person could only enter the Impossible City via the graveyard path once, which didn't make all that much sense, when she looked at it with open eyes. If a dead person taking a secret road into a City that didn't entirely seem to exist was impossible the first time, it ought to be impossible every single time after, or it wasn't playing fairly. Still, if she stumbled past the walls when they finally opened those doors to allow her companions entrance, she could find herself locked outside with the Army of the King of Cups, and no way to get back to her friends.

She could stand to be stranded in the Up-and-Under, she thought, as long as she didn't have to do it alone.

Both hats were looking at her now, their caterpillar heads twisted around at odd and painful-looking angles, their human hosts not moving so much as a muscle.

"She could be lying," said one hat. "Humans have been known to lie when they want things."

"But it's such a strange, *specific* lie," argued the other. "Humans only make up fantastic stories when they don't care about being believed. Human child!"

"Er, yes?" asked Zib.

"Do you care about being believed?"

"I mean . . . I guess not *all* of the time," said Zib.

172

She had the feeling, strange but sharp, that lying to these creatures would go very badly for her. Since she was already dead—or not "dead," exactly, as she understood the term to normally apply; she was fairly sure dead things weren't supposed to be up and moving around, but she was, and she could see the graveyard path and oh, it was so very confusing— she didn't want to find out how things could turn even worse. "Sometimes I just want to say stuff for the sake of saying stuff, like that I saw the shiniest rock or the biggest butterfly that anyone's ever seen in the whole world, but that's just silliness. When I'm being sincere, I want to be believed. When I say I brushed my teeth or—or put my shoes away, or did my homework."

As she explained those small instances of telling the truth in everyday ways, the realization that she was never going to do those things again, was never going to see her parents or sleep in her own bed or go to school with her friends loomed closer and closer, reaching out with tangled threads of understanding that she was still strong enough, for the moment, to shove aside.

"You never lie?" asked the other creature.

"I just told you I did, but not about things that *matter*. I'm not lying about *this*. The Queen of Wands is right outside, with the King of Cups and Jack Daw from the Kingdom of Swords and the Great Owl of Fire. Maybe the other owls too, by now. I don't know. I've been in here, and they're all out *there*, which is why I need you to open the doors." Zib stomped her foot again, harder this time, and for a moment it felt like her leg was going to break off her body and become something else entirely. She froze, trying to understand the sensation. It was like things were moving under her skin, like she was breaking into pieces while standing perfectly still.

It wasn't pleasant. She didn't like it. And at the same time, she could see how it might eventually become ordinary and everyday, something she would just accept without a second thought.

"What's lost if we open the doors?" asked the first creature, of the second.

"Oil from the hinges, muscle from the mounts," said the second. "What's gained?"

"If the human child speaks truly, an absent Queen and her companions, to set the tower light ablaze and put all right with the world," said the first. "What's the price?"

"A death, a life, a transformation," said the second. "If we open the doors, everything changes. The crown may pass. The war may begin. We have no way of knowing. Change is the price, as it has always been before, when the City gates have been opened. None are meant to pass in and out of the City but the reigning monarch, the lonely dead, and the watching light of the moon. This will change everything."

"If opening a door changes everything, maybe everything needed to be changed," said Zib.

The two creatures looked at each other for a long moment. Then they turned, as one, to look at Zib. Neither spoke. Zib fought not to squirm.

Finally, the two creatures turned away, pulling their long bodies downward until they were once again curled like woolly hats. They didn't stop there, but began to fully uncurl and inchworm their way down the long bodies of the men who had supported them. Each man, when his hat departed, was revealed to be missing the top portion of his head: instead, there was a shallow bowl, filled with nothing at all.

The creatures worked their way to either side of the gates.

"Change is neither good nor bad," said one. "Change simply *is*, and must be accepted as such."

"But not every change is forever," said the other. "Remember that, child of fire, child of feathers, child of humankind."

They rose to their full lengths then, caterpillars nearly as tall as Zib herself, and wrapped their front portions around a pair of tiny levers that had been concealed in the stone. They relaxed, allowing their weight to pull them downward, and the doors of the Impossible City swung open with a rusty, dusty creak, revealing the field beyond.

The army of the King of Cups was still there, but they no longer fought among themselves. Instead, they were arrayed in ranks, their weapons at the ready, and at their head stood the Page of Frozen Waters, a longer blade of that not-ice held in one hand, her cold eyes fixed on the now-open doors.

Between the army and the wall stood Zib's companions, sheltered by the wings of all four owls, who had landed at some point to surround them and cover them with feathers.

"The gates are open!" exclaimed Jack.

"Come on," shouted Zib.

"Advance," snapped the Page.

The army began to march forward, step by terrible step, as Zib's friends hurried away from the owls toward the open gate. The King of Cups moved with them, only little older than Jack in face, but still moving with the tight awareness of someone who was truly ancient.

Avery and Niamh looked terrified. Soleil, however, looked utterly and entirely serene, ushering the others along with her, never looking back. As she reached the threshold of the City, the owls took flight, their vast wings slapping at the sky.

"Hurry, now, children," she said. "All of you, hurry inside."

And Niamh, and Jack, and Avery stepped into the Impossible City.

Soleil paused, looking to the King of Cups. "You know why you're not welcome," she said, voice going gentle. "I would that you could be. I would that I could take you to my home, and feed you at my table, and shelter you beneath my roof. But we both understand that's not possible, even in the Impossible City. Two monarchs cannot carry a single crown."

The King of Cups said nothing, only looked at her with sad, grave eyes.

"If you step back, we can close the gates before the army your Page rose in your name reaches us," she said. "We can prevent this war. Or you can stay where you are, and we can cast the Up-and-Under into turmoil. The choice is yours."

Avery looked at Niamh, wide-eyed. "Why is she just standing there talking to him? There's an *army* coming! They have *swords!*"

"Yes, but until he enters, he hasn't challenged for the crown, and they can't come through the gates, however much they might want to," she said. "The Up-and-Under has rules all its own, and it enforces them without walls or fences. It's like the graveyard path. It's always open to the dead. So shouldn't it be easy for anyone who wants to claim the crown to train up an assassin, poison their tea, and dispatch them to the City for a little light regicide?"

"Regi-what?"

"Regicide is the killing of a ruling monarch," said Niamh, sounding faintly frustrated. "It's not the point; it's the act, and it's where one of the rules comes into play. The City protects its own. The citizens and the monarchy both. As long as the Queen of Wands is on her own ground, an opposing monarch can only enter with her consent. Anyone who belongs entirely and elementally to an opposing monarch can't enter at all. I can be here only because no one who began human can be entirely purely of one element or another."

"But you said—"

"I'm tired of trying to explain complicated things in simple ways so you can hear them," snapped Niamh. "If he comes into the City, he does so because she allowed him. His army will follow, because he is here, and a King cannot bar his own people from his side. The war will come with them, and all will fall."

The King of Cups sighed heavily. "I win," he said. "I always win."

"Yes, when the time is right for you to play," said Soleil. It was Soleil who spoke, but it was the Queen of Wands who leaned back over the threshold of the city to press a burning kiss against his forehead. "The wheel is not yet turning, my friend. Come again when the wind is in the west and the ground is wet with rain. Your turn at the dice will come."

The King of Cups bowed his head as the Queen of Wands straightened, safe within the Impossible City once more. Zib caught a glimpse of a blistered mark in the shape of a kiss where the Queen's lips had been. The Queen—still the Queen, scarce Soleil at all—raised a hand in imperious command, and the caterpillar-creatures wrapped themselves around the levers once again. This time they pushed, harder than should have been possible, and as the levers came down, the gates swung shut, leaving the four children and the Queen in the Impossible City.

FOURTEEN
THE TOWER FOUND

"This won't do at all," said the Queen of Wands crossly, looking around herself at the continuously shifting streets. Even the people were flickering like kinetoscope images, changing between one step and the next. None of them looked at the Queen and her companions. It was as if they, all of them, existed in some other, stranger story.

The two caterpillar creatures were the only ones to acknowledge her, inchworming their way along to settle by her feet and rear up, lifting half their fuzzy bodies off the cobblestones.

"The human child spoke truly," said one of them.

"The drowned girl told no lies," said the second.

"Welcome home, Your Majesty," they said in unison, and bowed to her before turning away and climbing back up the bodies of the guards, settling into position as fuzzy hats once more.

The Queen of Wands barely seemed to take notice of this strange production. She turned to face the others, and she still wasn't Soleil, but only and entirely the Queen. She sighed, as heavy as a gale, and clapped her hands.

All around them, the City froze. Even frozen, it continued to change; every building and body shifted and shimmered like a prism, too out of focus to see with any clarity. The only ones not so changed were the ones who had been her traveling companions on the road, who were not citizens, but only visitors there.

"That can hold them for a little while," said the Queen. "Come now, quickly onward. We'll be safe in my tower."

"Aren't we safe in your city?" asked Avery.

"Not yet," said the Queen. "Close enough for a harvest, not so precise as for a pie. Come along, come along." And with that, she began walking quickly away, moving between the frozen, glimmering people like they were nothing more than unwanted obstacles. The others followed, all in a line, and she never once paused or looked back to see where they had been or what had come before them.

Avery glanced down. The cobblestones beneath

her feet gleamed with slick rainbow light. Here, at the end of their journey, the improbable road had returned to them at last.

He didn't know whether that was reassuring or upsetting. For the road, which had abandoned them several times when they needed it most dearly, to come crawling back now felt—mean, somehow. Unfair, and a little bit like cheating. Why, this way the next travelers to find themselves in the Up-and-Under could also be told that the improbable road would see them all the way to their destination, and it wouldn't be a lie! There would just be no mention made of the places in the middle where they would be forced to walk alone, with no map and no compass to guide them.

Avery scowled and kept his sour thoughts to himself, following the Queen and the others until they were approaching a tall building built from a dozen different shades of quartz, from purest white to deepest black, all of them veined with flakes of sparkling silver and gold. It was a riot of color that should have been disharmonious and clashed with itself, and yet seemed perfectly seamless and correct instead, like a field of wildflowers, or a flawless sunset. There was only one door. It wasn't guarded.

Not hesitating, the Queen walked to the door and pulled it open, gesturing the rest of them inside. "The quarterly foundations are hard to speak or see, but we live as they would guide us, and their rigors set us free," she said, in the same tone the Page of Frozen Waters had used for her recitation. "Welcome to the heart of the Up-and-Under, children. Now hurry inside, and we'll have your story ended in a twinkle."

"I don't want to be over," said Zib anxiously. She plucked at the front of her shirt, where the flower of fire had burned. "I walked the graveyard path to get us here, but that doesn't mean I'm ready to be ended."

"A story and the self are not the same," said the Queen. "Any more than a shadow and the object that casts it are the same. Memory is a sort of story. If we all sat down on the tower steps and recited the things which have come thus far to one another, we would tell very different stories, and none of us would be entirely correct, and none of us would be lying. Now hurry, hurry. I need to reach the parlor and relight the beacon."

From above them came a long, slow tolling sound, as of some great clockwork striking the hour. The Queen's lips contorted in a frown.

"The clock is in the attic, chiming out the hour," she said. "Hurry."

Niamh was the first to step inside, followed closely by Jack, and then Avery and Zib, Zib glancing over her shoulder like she feared the closing door would cut off her last view of the world.

The Queen of Wands was the last one inside.

She closed the door, frowned still more deeply, said, "This won't do at all," and clapped her hands again.

With a terrible cracking sound, like ice on a frozen lake giving way to the thaw, she, along with three of her four companions, split in two. Only Avery was left untouched and staring.

When the crack faded, two people stood where the Queen of Wands had been: the Queen herself, and a younger girl, barely into her teens, with hair as red as a rose and a gown of brown hawk's feathers. Zib had been replaced by herself and a second, shadowy self whose hair was straight and combed, whose skin was pale, and whose fingers were streaked with ash. There were two Niamhs, one damp and one dry, and seeing her without moisture slicking down her hair was strange enough that she looked almost entirely unfamiliar. Jack seemed almost unchanged, save for the second boy standing beside him, who had a weight and a concreteness that he had never before possessed.

"There, that's better," said the Queen. "Come, children, to the stairs."

She resumed walking, and the others followed, even the redhaired girl in the hawk-feather gown.

None of them questioned what had just happened, although Avery was so full of questioning that he felt as if he might choke on it, might start gagging on unspoken words and unuttered syllables. Up and up and up they went, until the endless winding stair finally *did* come to an end, for nothing is truly endless, not even the improbable road.

At the top of the stairs—or whatever point along the stairs they had actually come to—was a round, pleasant parlor with a single window looking out on the rest of the Up-and-Under. A lamp was set there, currently extinguished. The Queen of Wands walked over to it, tapping the glass with the very tip of her index finger. It sprang at once to life, casting a warm white light over the room and outside at the same time.

From below them, a great and gleeful cheer rose up. The red-haired girl smiled. "And all is right with the world," she said, with profound relief.

"Perhaps." The Queen of Wands turned to face the group of them, all eight—when the three doubled children were counted alongside Avery and the red-haired girl—and sighed. "There is still the question of how this all ends."

"We go home," said Avery. "We go home, and this gets to be a story, and we get to be safe and with our parents, and grow up the way we're supposed to."

Zib nodded her agreement.

"But for some of you, this *is* home," said the Queen. "You were told that to find me would be to see your journey ended, and you found me despite all obstacles. You walked the improbable road to the

Impossible City, and I can grant you each one impossible thing, if you so desire."

"I want to go home," said Avery, with absolute conviction.

"I know," said the Queen. She looked to Niamh, and then at her dry twin. "What do you want, daughter of the depths? Your second self has never drowned."

"I don't know her," said Niamh. "I've never been her. I want to go home. The thaw is coming. Can I go home?"

"I can't go home," said Jack, and his more solid shadow sighed. "The Queen my mother will never forgive me what I've done. Can I stay here? Both of me?"

"No," she said. "Outside this tower, there is only one of you. But the one who exists outside may stay, and ever after."

Jack hesitated a moment before he nodded, expression grave. "Then I will renounce my ties to Air, and be only ever here, but still remain myself, as I am made and meant, and thank you for the opportunity to make my choices."

Zib, who had split like the two of them, but had as yet no idea what was going on, looked from Jack to Avery to her own second self, her evident confusion deepening with every glance. "I don't understand what this is," she said.

"It's impossible for a drowned girl to return to the city beneath the ice once she's missed the thaw, and yet she's to return there," said the Queen. "All she needs to do is leap from the tower window, to trust me one more time, and Meadowsweet will come to carry her home. And it's impossible for a son of Air to settle peacefully under a monarch of Fire, but as he wishes it so, he shall remain, and Broom will fly home empty-taloned. Your Avery will be carried home by Oak, who will come when he jumps. As to you . . ."

She glanced to the red-haired girl. "That comes down to my second self. If she chooses to run away again—which should be quite impossible, but this is a time and place where impossible things occur, and she was as key in getting me here as any of the rest of you—then Fern's talons are full. But if she chooses to stay, Fern can fly home another. And what's more impossible than a child of fire who snuffed herself out for her Queen, walked the graveyard path, and returned to the lands of the living?"

The red-haired girl looked at Zib and sighed, low and longing. In that sound was every day she wouldn't live, every road she wouldn't walk, every sky she wouldn't soar.

"Go home, Hepzibah," she said. "Go home and be well, and stay far away from the Up-and-Under."

"To the window now, quick, quick," said the Queen of Wands, and hurried them along, our last three travelers, leaving their shadow-selves and companions behind.

Niamh was first to be boosted onto the ledge. She looked solemnly at Avery. "I didn't expect to like you, at the start, but I found the way," she said. "Be better than you've been. Bend."

Then she pushed off, and she was falling, falling, without a single sound. In a rustle of wings, Meadowsweet swept by and upward, with Niamh clutched firmly in her talons. Niamh waved, and then she was gone, out of sight, leaving their tale forever.

Avery was next, for he was very anxious to go home. He screwed his eyes shut as he jumped, and was almost surprised when Oak's talons closed around his arms to stop his falling. He opened his eyes and looked up at the Great Owl, who hooted in soft acknowledgment and flew on, away from the tower, away from the City, faster and truer than ever the improbable road could have been.

In the tower, Zib hesitated. "I want to go home," she said slowly. "I want to see my parents. I want to be alive. But I don't want to never see the Up-and-Under again. Is that so wrong?"

"Not at all," said the Queen of Wands, "and when the time comes for you to continue your journey, we will welcome you—even Jack, whose advice was well meant, if impossible to accept. But for now, you must go, or the chance will pass you by."

Zib took a deep breath, hoisted herself onto the window ledge, and leapt, eyes open. Fern rose up to meet her, and in the grasp of the Great Owl of Fire, Zib soared away from the Impossible City. A flock of jackdaws spilled from the tower window, but was not fast enough to escort her, only fly along behind, dwindling swiftly into distance.

Then Fern was pulling up alongside Oak, and the two owls were soaring above a great forest. Broom came to fly beside them for a time, talons empty, until there was a wall, far, far below, gray stone across green brush, impossible and improbable and out of place.

The owls dipped lower, and as they brushed the air above the wall, they let the children go.

In the end, Avery and Zib fell only a few feet, landing hard but uninjured on the dusty ground.

FIFTEEN

AN IMPOSSIBLE STORY

Zib was the first to turn and look behind herself, and was unsurprised to see no wall, only a long street stretching off into the city. She felt her hip, and found no sword belted there. Flopping over backward in the street, she spread her arms, staring up at the sky, and began to laugh.

Avery blinked several times before he started laughing, too, and fell back to sprawl beside her, his head on her arm, his eyes on the clouds above them.

They were still laughing when the police, who had been looking for two missing children for the better part of a month, pulled up and gathered them from the road, whisking them away to the station

for mugs of cocoa and bowls of soup as their parents were called, passing on the good news of their return.

Neither Avery nor Zib could ever explain where they had been to the satisfaction of the adults in their lives. Zib was the first to give up on trying, recognizing that some stories are too impossible to ever be told. Avery tried longer, convinced that he had been honest long enough to be believed, but in the end, he fell to silence as well, and the two of them continued through their days, wary of walls, conscious of crows, and neither would ever trust another road to remain for as long as they lived.

And of course they eventually returned to the Up-and-Under, many times, together and apart. This would hardly be an impossible story if they didn't, now, would it? And this is, after all, an impossible story, whether this is your first time following it or your fiftieth. It was impossible until we told it together, and now it is nothing but lies, and nothing but the truth, and I am finished, I am finished, I am done; I shall rest now, content that I have done my duty.

The Queen is in her parlor, the light is in her tower: the clock is in the attic, chiming out the hour. And all the children wild and free and all the ladies pretty are putting on their dancing shoes and heading for the City.

Now rest, my dears, and be at ease; there's a fire

in the hearth and a wind in the eaves, and the night is so dark, and the dark is so deep, and it's time that all good little stars go to sleep.

I'll be waiting when you wake.

ACKNOWLEDGMENTS

Thank you to everyone who has helped me in the process of traveling the improbable road to the Impossible City, and beyond, into tales untold and dreams as yet undreamt of. We have come so far. We have, always and ever, so far left to go.

Most of all, thank you to James. I know you will do what you were made for.

I know you will finish what we started.

I remain, as I was ever,

Asphodel